A TOUCH OF MAGIC

Lorna is trying to rebuild her life after the war that robbed her of her husband and her son of a father he never knew. However, eleven-year-old Simon refuses to accept that Max is dead. Lorna does not believe in miracles, but it is Christmas and all Simon asks is the chance to see the place where his father's plane crashed. In the dense Basque forest, a man called Olentzero brings a touch of magic back into their lives . . .

Books are to be returned on or before
the last date below.

BLYTH

2 MAY 2017   2 3 MAR 2022

2 1 SEP 2017

                13 APR 2023

1 3 MAR 2018

- 7 AUG 2018
2 0 NOV 2018

2 3 JAN 2019

1 5 JUN 2019

2 1 JUN 2019

1 6 FEB 2022

www.librex.co.uk

JUNE GADSBY

A TOUCH OF MAGIC

Complete and Unabridged

LINFORD
Leicester

First published in Great Britain in 2008

First Linford Edition
published 2009

British Library CIP Data

Gadsby, June.
A touch of magic- -(Linford romance library)
1. War widows- -Fiction. 2. Children of war
casualties- -Fiction. 3. Love stories.
4. Large type books.
I. Title II. Series
823.9′2–dc22

ISBN 978–1–84782–867–5

Published by
F. A. Thorpe (Publishing)
Anstey, Leicestershire

Set by Words & Graphics Ltd.
Anstey, Leicestershire
Printed and bound in Great Britain by
T. J. International Ltd., Padstow, Cornwall

This book is printed on acid-free paper

A Hope Undimmed

'But I don't want to go skiing in the Alps!' Lorna's son said in a petulant voice. It was uncharacteristic behaviour from her normally good-natured child. She was a little worried about him. The mood swings had started a few weeks ago. She had tried to ignore them, hoping they would go away. They hadn't.

There was a patient, low-voiced response from David. It was met by a loud 'No!' from Simon and then a door banged. Footsteps thudded on the stairs followed by an uncomfortable silence. Lorna sighed. She was quite at a loss to understand why Simon was reacting so violently to David's offer to take them all to Switzerland for Christmas. It was a very generous offer from someone who was not yet her husband.

Ordinarily, she thought that Simon, as she herself had done, would have been jumping for joy at such a prospect. Not many people could afford to travel far these days, and especially not abroad. It may be 1951, and the war may have been over for six years, but the aftermath was still being felt.

And yet Simon had responded to David's generous and exciting suggestion with a brooding silence.

David had been a part of their lives for over two years now, during which time he had been a model surrogate father. Simon had quickly become fond of the new man in his mother's life. That is, until recently, when things had changed, seemingly overnight.

Normally calm and well-behaved, Simon had become moody and sharp-tempered and Lorna was more worried about him than she dared to admit. Her friends assured her, speaking from their own experience, that it was nothing more than 'a phase'.

Lorna's mother had diagnosed 'growing pains' and assured her daughter that Simon would grow out of it. Lorna had argued that eleven was surely too young for these so-called 'growing pains'.

'He's probably precocious, just like his grandfather,' her mother had said, and went on to reminisce about the days of her husband's youth, with a tear of nostalgia for that golden era before the war.

Her parents' marriage was happy, and, Lorna thought with a sigh, at least they still had each other.

She picked up the tea tray she had been preparing and took it into the living room. David, always impeccably mannered, rose and took the tray from her. He was frowning, but with his typical patience he waited for her to broach the subject of Simon.

★   ★   ★

'What was all that about?' Lorna asked, handing David his cup and offering him a piece of his favourite cherry Genoa cake. It was still warm from the oven and filled the whole house with a buttery, fruity, mouth-watering aroma.

David shrugged and then smiled in delight as he bit into the cake, savouring it as if it were laced with nectar of the gods.

'You really must let my mother have the recipe for this,' he said, not for the first time.

His mother. If that woman had had her way, they would have been married long ago. However, there was always something inside Lorna that stopped David every time they got close to the question of marriage. It was like a heavy door slamming in the dark recesses of her mind. The fact that they had never found Max's body had a lot to do with it.

'You didn't answer my question, David,' she said, ignoring his request for the cake recipe, which she suspected was a ploy to veer the conversation away from Simon.

'What question was that?'

'I thought I heard you and Simon arguing. I certainly heard my son's voice raised.' Lorna lifted an enquiring eyebrow. 'My son, who used to be your best pal and seems to have fallen out with you?'

'Oh, that . . . yes.'

David looked uncomfortable. He gazed at a point beyond her shoulder and tugged at his left ear, so she knew something was bothering him. After years of being his colleague, his friend and, more lately, his girlfriend, she could read him like the proverbial open book. Which was apt, since they worked together in the local library.

'Well? Are you going to tell me, or is it a State Secret?' She showed him her mischievous, dimpled smile that he had helped her find again.

'Nothing too serious,' David assured her, though his eyes said something else. 'Simon says he won't go to Switzerland and there doesn't appear to be any room for negotiation.'

'I wonder if he's scared of going on the slopes. Neither of us has skied before, although I think it's a lovely idea. Simon's always been fond of snow and he's fascinated by mountains. He's always reading about them.'

'Ah, yes . . . ' David cleared his throat. 'I think it's rather more than not wanting to go to Switzerland to ski.'

'Meaning?' Lorna looked at David over the rim of her tea cup, dreading what he was about to divulge. What could possibly be upsetting her happy, stable son who had not given her a day's anxiety until now?

'They're the wrong mountains,' David said.

'The wrong mountains?'

'Yes. And the wrong country and, I'm afraid . . . the wrong man.'

'The wrong man?' Gracious, she was beginning to sound like a parrot the way she was repeating things, but Lorna hardly dared give credence to the thoughts that were going through her head.

Her heart dipped slightly as David reached out and took her hand in both of his.

'Darling Lorna,' he said gently, and something heavy descended from her heart to the pit of her stomach. 'I love you very much, and I'm extremely fond of the lad, but as long as he believes that his father might still be alive . . . '

'Oh, David, not that again,' said Lorna, pulling her hand away and getting up to pace the room. 'I thought he got over that business ages ago.'

'Afraid not. Lorna, do you think . . . you know . . . that Simon needs help?'

She rounded on him, a mother quick to jump to the defence of her offspring. How dare he suggest there was something wrong with her son? He was the most well adjusted boy in his class, despite never having had a father's support and influence. His teachers all said he was a model pupil and a credit to her. Single parents didn't always succeed too well, it seemed. Well, she had made sure that Simon had all that was necessary to lead a happy, healthy life. The fact that he didn't have a father was not her fault. Or his.

She pulled her hand away and stared disbelievingly into David's blue eyes. She couldn't recall ever being angry with him, but his words had lit a fuse somewhere inside her.

'A psychiatrist, do you mean?' The cold tone of her voice told him exactly what she thought of his remark. 'David, there's absolutely nothing wrong with Simon. He's a normal, healthy boy.'

But for once, David was not going to be swayed.

'It's not healthy to be so fixated on the idea of finding a man who was reported missing, believed dead. For goodness' sake, Lorna, it's been nearly twelve years.'

'Yes,' she said, dully. 'I know.'

She had counted every single year, month, week, day since Max had gone missing. And she went on counting, and missing him, because they had never found him. Not even a trace.

'It's not as if Simon ever knew his father,' David said gently.

'No, that's true.'

Lorna lowered her eyes and concentrated on her thumbnail. Poor, dear Max. He had been drawn into the war from day one. It wasn't going to be dangerous, he assured her time and time again. He was a musician and, like many others who played instruments or sang or acted, his talents would not be wasted on fighting. He was going out there to entertain the troops. Nothing more than that.

He considered it to be his duty and, she was sure, he even saw it as an exciting period in his otherwise happy and successful life. And he had further assured her that he would be quite safe.

*   *   *

Lorna had fallen head over heels in love with the tall, good-looking violinist the first time they met. And when she heard the beautiful, wistful music he played, she was completely captivated.

Maxwell Barrett was already world famous by then. He had an incredible aura of power that exuded from him. Men admired him. Women adored him. Yet, despite all the adoration, it was well known that he lived only for his music. That is, until he walked into the library, met Lorna, and made her the most important part of his world. More important than his music, he had told her. The expression in his dark eyes when he told her that, was so genuine, she believed him. Max was the kind of man you just believed, and believed in.

'Don't you go worrying,' he had said as he kissed her goodbye. 'I'll be back.'

Then off he went, looking impressive and even more handsome in his captain's uniform. He took with him the violin his father had made for him when he was a boy not much older than Simon. His prized Stradivarius he left with Lorna for safekeeping.

'Please keep him safe!' Lorna had prayed silently. It was a prayer she had said countless times, even after people told her to give up.

* * *

Max's plane went down somewhere in the Pyrenees in a raging storm. They had been heading for Toulouse, but got blown off course. Rescue workers, mainly French and Spanish Basques, searched high and low, but found no sign of the plane or its occupants. And Lorna got the telegram every wife and mother dreaded, telling her of his disappearance. It was the same day the doctor had confirmed that she was carrying their child.

A light touch on Lorna's arm made her start. She dragged her mind away from the memory of Max's beloved face and the way he had looked the last time she had seen him.

* * *

'Can't you talk to the lad again, Lorna?' A look of desperation had crept into

11

David's eyes. 'I mean, everything was fine between us until he saw that newspaper report about the piece of fuselage being found. You and I both know that even if they launch a new search, they're not going to find anyone. Nobody survived that crash, or we would have known about it.'

Lorna felt a lump rising in her throat. The sudden, unexpected flood of emotion had brought tears to eyes that she thought could never cry again over the one man she had ever truly loved. And still loved to this day. Sometimes, the feelings she had for Max seemed just as strong as they had ever been. When that happened, she had to remind herself that he was no longer here.

Maybe that was the problem. Deep down inside her, she had never stopped loving Max. And when the journalists and the wireless reporters resurrected the great violinist, Maxwell Barrett, printing his photograph and playing some of his better-known recordings,

Simon had suddenly wanted to know more and more about his missing father, plying her daily with questions, never letting the subject rest for long.

'I'll talk to Simon later,' she told David. 'After you've gone home.'

'Well, I hope you have better luck than I did,' David said with a sigh. 'I tried every trick in the book, including blackmail.'

'Blackmail!' Lorna laughed. 'What on earth did you blackmail him with? He's a little saint and you know it.'

'Well, I wouldn't go so far as to call him a saint.' David was laughing too, obviously as glad as she was that the mood had lightened. 'Poor little mite. Being a saint is a terrible responsibility and not one I would wish on my worst enemy.'

'All right, come on, tell me,' she said. 'What did you try and bribe him with?'

'Nothing out of the ordinary.'

'You didn't offer him money, I hope,' Lorna gave him a disapproving look.

'Afraid I did.'

'And?'

'It didn't impress him one little bit.'

'Well, I'm glad to hear it. I'd hate to think I'd raised a boy that could be bribed. My son has strong principles.'

'He's as stubborn as a mule.' David gave a wry smile. 'Nothing will shake him free of the idea that his father might still be alive.'

Maybe, Lorna thought, a part of her also wanted to believe that Max was still alive out there somewhere, however much the sensible side of her brain told her this was an impossible dream.

But how could she convince an eleven-year-old to recognise it as such?

★   ★   ★

Simon was giving her that hurt look that she had come to know only too well. He was like his father in so many ways. Not only physically. They shared the same passion for music, and the violin in particular. And, exasperating though it was, Simon was every bit as stubborn as Max had been once he got his mind set on something.

'Look, sweetheart, this is very difficult for me,' she said, not quite sure how to handle the subject. 'I wish your father was still alive, too, but he isn't.'

'How do you know, Mum? He might still be out there somewhere, lost and alone and wishing that somebody would come and find him.'

Lorna sighed and there was a catch in her throat as she continued, 'Simon, your father was a very clever, intelligent man. If he were alive somewhere, we would have known about it. He would have got back to us somehow.'

'But maybe . . . ' Simon dried up and he too heaved a disconsolate sigh.

'It's twelve years since he disappeared.' She reached out and pulled her son into the circle of her arms, hugging him tightly, and for once, he didn't blush and squirm. 'Darling, it would make me the happiest person in the world to have him come back, but it's not possible. Only a miracle would bring him back to us and . . . well, I'm sorry, Simon, but I don't believe in miracles. Not any more.'

Why did her heart not agree with her head? Because, if she was honest, she had to admit she had secretly never stopped hoping. In the beginning it was a matter of believing every day that her beloved Max would be found and returned safely to her. Then the weeks went by, dragging on into months and years. Her heart had not only been broken, it had been shattered without any hope of being mended.

That is, until she met David. He had walked into her life and saved her. He had made her smile again, given her life new meaning. She no longer tried to get through each day as it came, shutting out the pain, the loneliness.

And David was good with Simon, too. That was almost the best part of the relationship.

★   ★   ★

Simon, not about to give up, was tugging at her sleeve.

'We could go to France and make sure, couldn't we? Please, Mum!'

'Oh, Simon . . . ' She shook her head slowly. They had been offered the chance to go over and see the area where the plane had possibly gone down, but Lorna had declined. Somehow she couldn't see herself laying a wreath for her dead husband in that vast, wild countryside without knowing for certain that he was there.

Simon pushed away from Lorna and she saw streaks of glistening tears on his cheeks. How can the boy grieve so much for a father he has never known? Lorna asked herself. All he had ever known about Max were the photographs she had saved for him and a collection of records that he had played over and over since he was of an age to appreciate music. The records were all scratchy now, but he still listened to them on Max's old gramophone.

'I don't think that going to France

would do any good, Simon.' She hated to sound so negative. 'Besides, David has already booked the tickets to go to Switzerland. It's beautiful over there. I'm sure you'll love it.'

'I don't care what David has done.' Simon's cheeks were suddenly suffused with angry red patches. 'My dad's not in Switzerland. He's still in France where his plane crashed. He's in the mountains.'

Lorna shook her head. He sounded so positive she almost believed him. And oh, how she wished it were true. She had found it hard to accept that Max was no longer a part of her world. There had been no body, no burial, only a very moving memorial service attended by friends and relatives. The church had been full to overflowing. Outside, thousands of his admirers had gathered to pay homage to the great Maxwell Barrett. The whole occasion had been beautifully handled, yet it had been quite unreal.

'I dreamed of my dad the other

night,' Simon said, his back to her, his shoulders hunched, as he looked at his favourite photograph of his father. 'He was playing his violin and he was calling out to me, but I couldn't understand what he was saying.'

'It was just a dream, sweetheart,' Lorna told him. 'Dreams aren't real. As soon as we wake up the dreams disappear, just like a bubble bursting.'

'Do you ever dream of him?' He was regarding her intently.

'All the time,' Lorna told him, a catch in her throat.

It was the truth. Hardly a night went by without Max occupying a small but significant place in her thoughts and dreams.

'David's all right, you know,' Simon said suddenly. He put down his father's photograph and picked up the violin he had been practising on since he was old enough to hold it steady under his chin. 'I do like him, actually.'

'I know you do, Simon,' Lorna said. 'That's why I don't understand why you're making things so difficult for him right now.'

'I don't mind you being his friend,' he said slowly. 'But you can't marry him, because you're still married to my father.'

Without looking at his mother, he raised the violin and positioned it carefully on his shoulder, tucking his chin well in. Then, with careful precision, he drew the bow over the instrument's taught strings, making it come alive.

How could she explain to this wide-eyed, innocent child of hers that she needed to draw a line across the past? Her life had to move forward, preferably with David. The thing was, could she do it, without proper closure?

The telephone ringing in the hall downstairs saved her from further difficult moments with her son. She kissed Simon awkwardly on the top of his head as he sat in the window seat of his room, exactly as Max used to sit when he practiced the more difficult tunes in his wide repertoire.

It caused Simon to play a discordant note, but he went on without complaint.

★   ★   ★

Downstairs, Lorna picked up the telephone.

'Lorna, I've maybe made a huge mistake,' David's voice said in her ear.

'David? What are you talking about?' Lorna's stomach churned as she anticipated bad news.

But that wasn't the case, as David's next words proved.

'I've been to the travel agent and changed our booking.'

'You've done what?'

There was a slight hesitation, then David went on, a little uncertainly, 'I could live to regret this, Lorna, but tell Simon that he can have his wish. We're not going to Switzerland after all. We're going to France.'

'The Pyrenees?' Lorna's heart rose and sank within the space of the same brief second.

'We can go by car. I've got all the maps. There are ski stations over there, too, so while you and that son of yours go ghost hunting, I can at least pass my time pleasurably, unless you insist on my accompanying you every minute.'

'Oh, David, you're wonderful!' Lorna cried down the phone at him. 'I can't believe you're doing this for Simon.'

'It's not just for Simon, though, is it? You need to get Max out of your system, too. Then . . . well, we'll see. Maybe we'll finally be able to move our lives forward. All three of us.'

He was right. Of course he was right. The drawing of that final line between the past and the present was all that was preventing her from going through the door to the future, where she could plant new roots that would grow and flourish. As long as she had the ghost of her dead husband lurking in her mind, she could not lay the foundations for the future.

'I'd be a fool not to love you, David,' she said, and meant it.

'Then make sure you never stop,' came the soft reply in her ear. 'Now, off you go and tell that boy of yours he can stop sulking.'

From Simon's room a wistful violin concerto drifted down to her. It was Max's favourite piece, the one that had made him famous. And it was Simon who was playing it, stumbling here and there, but oh, how Lorna wished that Max could hear his son perform. At his tender age, Simon had a long way to go before he found that touch of magic his father had possessed. But he would get there, and she would do everything in her power to help him on his way.

'Simon!' Lorna called up the stairs, unable to keep the excitement out of her voice. 'Simon, I've got some good news for you!'

Arriving in France

'How's your French, young man?'
Simon, who had been watching rows of
majestic plane trees sliding by on the
long, winding roads, responded to
David's question casually. He wasn't
about to show off in front of his
mother's friend, though Lorna knew
that her son was surprisingly good at
French, limited though it was. He had
been having private lessons for over a
year with a retired grammar school
teacher who lived nearby.

'I taught his father, so why not
Simon, eh?' old Mr Graham had said.
'It'll give me something to do and it
won't be an onerous task. He's a
surprisingly gifted child. Takes after
Max. If I'm any judge, he'll go far.'

Mr Graham had been teaching and
judging children for forty years, but it
didn't need him to tell Lorna what her

24

son was like. There was no doubt in her mind that Simon had what it took to be a success in any chosen occupation.

'I think he probably speaks the language better than I do,' she now told David, who was fluent because of his frequent trips to the Swiss Alps.

The war had put paid to those annual visits to the ski slopes. Now, he clearly couldn't wait to get back there again. His enthusiasm was infectious, even though they were heading for France rather than his beloved Switzerland.

'I'm really grateful to you for this, David,' Lorna said.

He reached over and squeezed her hand.

'I shall expect my reward when we get back to England. Maybe by then you'll be ready to become Mrs David Groves.'

She smiled back at him warmly, but at that moment her son chose to butt in and change the subject.

'How long are we going to be in

France?' he said from the back seat, where he was snuggled down warmly among their jackets and a supply of woollen blankets.

'Until the New Year,' David told him. 'Three weeks in all. That long enough for you, Simon?'

There was a weighty silence and Lorna glanced at Simon through the rear-view mirror of David's Austin Cambridge.

'I don't know,' came the small voice from the rear.

Lorna and David exchanged glances. Neither of them quite knew what to expect during this holiday, but they were prepared to go along with Simon's wishes wherever possible. And for as long as the holiday lasted. After that, they were agreed, it had to stop somehow, this overriding obsession with finding Max. If it didn't stop, then she would have to do what David suggested and seek expert help. She hated the thought of consulting a psychiatrist. There was such a stigma attached to it. However, failing all else, what could she do?

Lorna turned in her seat and regarded her son.

'Are you all right, sweetheart? You're not cold, are you?' She would have been surprised if the boy said that he was cold, since he was wearing about three layers of clothes and was covered by the fur coat David had insisted on buying her last Christmas.

Lorna had accepted the coat with bad grace. She would have preferred it if the beavers, who had been sacrificed in the manufacturing of it, were still running about happily. She was of the opinion that the best place for a beaver coat was on the beaver. Animal lover Max would have been appalled.

David, however, had meant well and she was loath to hurt his feelings, so she had forgiven him and now had to admit that she was going to be glad of the coat's warmth when they got to the Pyrenees.

'I'm all right, Mum.' Simon answered

her question with a long, bored sigh. 'How long will it be before we get there? David? How long?' Simon persisted.

David glanced at his watch and, in doing so, almost landed them in a ditch as the car hit a patch of mud and skidded dangerously.

'Sorry about that,' he said, getting the wheels back under control. 'These French roads are pretty lethal.'

* * *

They had been travelling for three days, making regular stops. They passed through places that Lorna had only vaguely heard of — Abbeville, Rouen, Alençon, Le Mans. The country was still visibly recovering from the war, with some villages and towns surviving the best they could around the rubble of bombed-out buildings that must once have looked so beautiful.

Their journey had taken them through Tours, Poitiers, Bordeaux and Bayonne, the scenery changing with every mile.

'How long now?' Simon persisted, emerging from his warm cocoon because the afternoon sun had heat in it and the frozen roads of the northern half of the country had been left behind some time ago.

'Not long now,' David said. 'Relax, son. We'll be there soon enough.'

'Yes, Simon.' Lorna gave him a warning glance. 'You must be patient. Sit back and enjoy the scenery. Look how beautiful it is here.'

She saw Simon turn his head to gaze out of the window. His expression remained totally blank.

The area they were driving through was wildly breathtaking rather than pretty. It was unbelievably green and well wooded. Rolling emerald hillsides rose to high cliffs and, beyond, the rugged snow-capped mountains of the Pyrenees pierced the blue sky and faded into the misty distance.

'We are going to go to that place, aren't we?' Simon asked, as David pulled into a surprisingly attractive *auberge* as the light started to fade and the sun bathed the land in a rosy glow.

'What place is that?' David got out of the car and stretched his stiff limbs. It had been a long, hard drive on unforgiving roads, even if the scenery had been magnificent.

'You know.' Simon got out of the car and kicked at a stone, raising a cloud of dust that was caught by a fresh breeze and whipped away like rust-coloured smoke. 'The place where my father's plane came down.'

'Well, we don't know where it came down exactly.' David frowned and sank his hands deep into his trouser pockets. The subject made him uncomfortable, as Lorna knew only too well. She wished her son would let it drop before David's patience was pushed beyond its limit.

'Yes we do!' Simon argued, his young voice rising to a squeak of indignation. 'They found a piece of it in the forest . . . the one with the funny name.'

'Forêt d'Iraty', Simon nodded.

'Can we go there? Can we, David? Mum, we've got to go there. Tell him, please.'

Her son gazed up plaintively into her face, and suddenly she knew exactly how Max must have looked as a boy. The likeness was so strong and getting stronger with every passing year.

'David knows why we've come here, darling,' she said gently. 'He's been kind enough to give up his Switzerland trip to bring us here to the Basque country. So don't get impatient with him. And it's a vast wilderness out there where your father's plane crashed. Even if we find the village near where it came down, there's no guarantee . . . '

'I know, but we have to try, don't we? We have to look for him.'

'It's doubtful that we'll find anything, Simon. And even if we do find some tiny piece of evidence that your father was there, that's all we're likely to find.'

Lorna closed her eyes and gave a little shake of her head. She had lost count of the number of times she had repeated those same words to her son. But still, she thought, they didn't seem to sink in. She could tell Simon the same thing till she was blue in the face and it wouldn't have any effect.

Simon looked towards the high mountains.

'My father is out there,' he said in the most mature voice Lorna had ever heard from an eleven-year-old. 'He's still alive. I know he is. He's just got to be, Mum. He's got to be!'

Lorna felt the hairs on her arms and the back of her neck rise as he spoke. She wished with all her might that there could be some truth in what Simon believed, but she knew that he was going to be disappointed. No man could survive a plane crash and live on for so many years without his existence being known to the local people and the authorities.

If Max were out there somewhere, he would be long since buried by years of shifting earth. There had been time for a young tree to sprout up over the spot where he lay. It would be a fitting epitaph for a man who loved nature. She wondered if Pyrenean winds whistled his favourite tunes, and if the birds sang sweeter in that place than anywhere else in the forest. How she would like to believe that. A man like Max, who had that touch of magic about him, ought not to have died in vain.

Lorna fought back the tears her thoughts had provoked. It seemed she stood there for a long time, locked into the memory of the past, clinging to it. Maybe she wasn't ready to marry someone else, after all. As long as she held on to her love for Max, no other man really stood a chance.

And yet she did love David. He was good and true, honest and kind. How could she not love him? She owed him so much.

★　★　★

David emerged from the low doorway of the Old Wattle And Daub Inn with a broad smile on his face. 'Come on, you two,' he said, 'they've got two rooms vacant, so I've booked us in for the night. And with the greatest of difficulty, I might add. The old lady speaks the strangest dialect I've ever come across. I couldn't understand anything she said. It's a mixture of French and Spanish by the sound of it, so I assume it's Basque.'

'Is there a bathroom?' Lorna asked and saw David's face twitch slightly in amusement.

'There's a space that passes for a bathroom with the biggest bath you ever did see, but I get the feeling that unless you want to wash in cold water, the hot water has to be boiled up on the stove in the kitchen.'

'Wonderful,' Lorna sighed, already feeling homesick and wondering how she was ever going to survive the lack of amenities in this poor land where only the rich in the cities knew any form of luxury. 'What about the beds?'

'Big and comfortable with musical springs. Looks clean enough, anyway, and Madame is already cooking up a big pot of something she calls *garbure* for supper.'

David caught sight of Simon's scowl of disgust and laughed. 'Don't worry. It's some kind of meat and vegetable soup, and it smells delicious. Okay, grab what you need and let's get settled in. I expect it gets pretty cold up here at night, so make sure you've got extra clothes.'

★　★　★

The garbure was, indeed, delicious. They managed two bowlfuls each, along with chunks of crusty bread and portions of strong, but creamy, sheep's cheese. Lorna and David washed theirs down with a glass of red house wine, while Simon drank some goat's milk, and surprised Lorna by declaring it good and asking for more.

Their hostess chatted all the way through the meal, only occasionally saying something her guests could understand. She was cheerful enough, though bossed her farmer husband about until he took himself out to the barn to smoke a Camel.

Lorna shared a room with Simon, for which she was more than a little grateful, since the temperature dropped to below zero in the night, with soughing winds that came at them from the mountains, taunting the cowbone chimes that hung from the ancient, gnarled, twisted stems of the leafless wisteria outside. The climber would burst into cones of lilac flowers in the spring, but for now the twigs and branches were black and bare.

'Mum? You awake?'

Simon spoke into the impenetrable darkness. His whisper caught Lorna just as she was drifting off to sleep.

'I am now,' she told him drowsily. 'Can't you sleep?'

'No. I keep thinking about my father.'

'Simon . . . ' Lorna wasn't totally sure where he was going; but she felt the need to soften any blow that might be heading her son's way, a blow that could crush him beyond repair.

'I know what you're going to say,' Simon said, putting a halt to her words before they formed on her lips. 'You don't believe that he's still alive, do you?'

'It's not that, Simon. It's just . . . Oh, you're far too young to understand, darling.'

'No, I'm not.'

'All right,' she said with a sigh of resignation. 'The fact is, Simon, I would love to believe that Max . . . that your father . . . is still alive. But I daren't think like that, because I . . . I couldn't bear to be proved wrong.'

In the stillness that followed, Lorna listened to her son's breathing against the silence of the black velvet night.

'Do you still love him?' The question was voiced so low she barely heard it.

'I'll always love him, Simon. Just as

I'll always love you, because you're my son . . . and the son of Maxwell Barrett, the best man that ever lived.'

'I love you, too, Mum.' She could tell he was almost asleep. 'But please don't marry David.'

'I thought you liked him?'

How many times were they to have this same conversation, she asked herself wearily.

'I do. He's all right, but . . . '

Lorna never found out the rest. Simon heaved a great sigh, and then his breathing evened out as he drifted off to sleep.

She turned on her side and faced the window. There were no curtains to shut out the light of the moon, or the twinkling stars, or the great swathe of stardust that made up the Milky Way. She didn't mind. It looked like an enchanted world out there.

Had Max been lucky enough to see such a night as this, she wondered, before he died? Her throat tightened and she squeezed her eyes firmly shut.

Oh, Max, Max, what happened to you all those years ago? The words she had repeated inside her head time and time again over the years were still the same. Whatever happened, I hope you died knowing that I loved you and that, somehow, you knew how strong that love was. There isn't anything that could destroy it, Max. No matter what happens.

As sleep finally overtook her, the jingling chimes on the terrace softened and distorted, until she thought she could hear a violin playing somewhere far off. And the violinist was playing a bittersweet melody that he had dedicated especially to her, the woman he had fallen in love with so long ago.

And, as the moving shadows of that strange room melted into one, she fancied she heard Max's voice calling to her, as if it came from the heart of the highest mountain that rose tall and majestic, piercing the sky and casting a protective shadow over the land. The sound echoed through her head as if carried on a caressing breeze.

'*Lorna! Lorna, my love . . .* '

She shivered.

'*Lorna! Lorna, I'm here!*'

The voice rang out stridently in her ears. She sat bolt upright in the bed, her heart banging fearfully in her chest.

The air in the room had a touch of ice in it. She struggled to see through the darkness, but all was still. After a moment, she lay back and pulled the coarse woollen blankets and heavy eiderdown up to her chin. It had been nothing but a dream. Max, her dear, sweet Max, was no more, except in her memory.

But the sound of his voice had seemed so real. As she drifted into a restless slumber, Lorna was almost ready to believe that her son was right. Max *was* alive somewhere, and in the next three weeks they would find him . . .

Lorna turned on her side and gazed at one star, bigger and brighter than all the others. It was twinkling at her as if it were a real live thing. It seemed so big and close she felt she could reach out and grasp hold of it. As she drifted off into a deeper slumber she felt almost like a child again, wishing on a star and believing that her wish would come true.

A Perilous Journey

After a breakfast of stale bread, which they dipped in bowls of steaming café au lait, they piled into the car and headed deeper into the Basque country.

The owner of the auberge drew David a sketchy map, while Lorna enjoyed a few moments in the fresh air, her face turned up to the sun to feel its gentle warmth.

The man jabbed a stubby finger at the name of the village he had written and repeated it several times.

'Mendibel,' he said, prodding and nodding knowledgeably. 'Mendibel. You go there.'

'And the forest where the plane was found?'

The Frenchman blew out his cheeks and shook his head. 'No plane. Only bits. Not here at Mendibel.' His hand moved and he jabbed again an inch or two further over to the west. 'Forest of Iraty. Is big. Many trees. No find plane. Is impossible.'

David thanked him anyway and they all piled into the car, driving until the auberge was out of sight. Then David stopped the car and consulted the map again.

'I don't think we should even contemplate going up there,' he said.

There was an exclamation of disbelief from Simon.

Lorna leaned over and tried to see the map through the clouds of steam that her breath was creating in the unheated vehicle. She was bitterly cold and wishing that she had packed warmer clothes.

'Where is this village?' she asked David.

'It's not even on the map, but it's apparently just south of St Jean Pied de Port . . . ' he searched the map then pointed at a spot he had marked. 'There. It's about as isolated as you can get in these parts. High up and tucked away in the middle of a dense forest. The farmer at the auberge said it wasn't a place for tourists. They say there are bears roaming all over the Pyrenees.'

'That's super!' Simon was suddenly sitting up and taking notice at the possibility of an encounter with a bear.

'What do you think?' Lorna said. 'Can we make it?'

'I'm not sure, Lorna. This car of mine has seen better days and the roads, if they exist at all, will be pretty treacherous. In fact, they're no more than dirt tracks for most of the way from here.'

'We're not going back!' Simon shouted the words from the back seat. 'We can't!'

'Hush, Simon,' Lorna said. 'We may have no choice, and since David has already sacrificed a lot for us, it's up to him what we do.'

'But he doesn't want us to find my father! He wants my dad to be dead so he can marry you.'

It was the first time Simon had ever

referred to Max as his 'dad'. Lorna glanced up at David and saw his cheek muscles tighten. What Simon had said just now had hit a raw nerve. Although he wouldn't admit to it, David almost certainly was not praying for a miracle. He did, however, want closure as badly as she did. Perhaps more than she did.

'David . . . ?' She touched his arm. 'If you don't want to go on, it's all right, really it is.'

He squared his shoulders and folded the map away.

'We'll go on,' he said, and Simon's relief was tangible.

'Thank you,' she said, giving him a grateful smile.

There was a moment's pause, then he nodded back to her as he put the car into gear and they set off on the final leg of their journey.

* * *

St Jean Pied de Port was an ancient, picturesque town. With its tall houses, their wooden balconies hanging over the river Nive that flowed through the centre, it might have belonged in a children's fairytale. The water, rippling over stones, twinkled in the winter sunshine like liquid diamonds. Red-masked Muscovy ducks dabbled among the weeds on the bank, and pied wagtails bobbed among the stones.

'Interesting place,' David said, as they coasted slowly along, looking for somewhere to stay, for it was unlikely they would find anything in the tiny hamlet of Mendibel.

'I'd like to see it in summer,' Lorna said, trying to imagine blue summer skies and scarlet geraniums tumbling from the window boxes beneath the quaint old windows and undulating red-tiled roofs.

'The book says it's the heart of the Basque country,' Simon piped up, lifting his head from the guidebook he was studying avidly. 'It's on the route of the Compostela pilgrim trail and, just over there . . . ' He waved a vague hand in the direction of the nearby mountain peaks, ' . . . is Spain.'

'He sounds like a courier in the making,' David said with an amused grin, as pleased as Lorna was to hear Simon taking more of an interest in their surroundings.

'What's a courier?' Simon wanted to know.

'A tourist guide.'

'Ugh! No way!' Simon was most indignant. 'I'm going to be a musician.'

★　★　★

They put up at a rather grand-looking manor house that had seen better days. It called itself the Hotel des Pyrenecs and appeared to be the only place offering accommodation.

'It is the war!' The proprietor raised his shoulders and turned his hands palm up in the traditional Gallic shrug. 'Nobody has the holidays any more.' His English was exceptionally good, for which they were thankful.

47

He showed them to what he proudly announced were the two best rooms and was surprised to find that Lorna and David had no intention of sharing.

'Ooh, la! Mes excuses! I thought that you were married. But now I make you the special price. The petit, he can have a room for himself. yes. And I give you, monsieur, madame, my two best rooms, no extra charge.'

They ate a surprisingly good lunch in the hotel dining room, then spent the rest of the remaining daylight hours exploring the old town.

Simon was anxious to move on, but even he was tired after the long journey from Calais, so he contained his impatience.

★   ★   ★

After supper, they were all three of them ready to go to bed. Lorna settled Simon into his room. He was asleep almost before his head touched the pillow, so she tiptoed out, leaving him with just a small night-light.

David was waiting outside her door. She wasn't quite sure how to read his expression and approached him a little hesitantly.

'Lorna . . . ' He murmured her name and something stabbed at her heart.

'Simon's asleep already,' she said, smiling brightly and fumbling for the large room key in her bag. 'I think the last three days are catching up on all of us. I know I'm totally exhausted and you must be too.' Why on earth was she rambling on like this?

David didn't speak, but took the key from her and opened her door.

'Thank you, David,' Lorna said hastily. 'Thank you for everything.'

'Lorna, I love you so much, you know.'

'I know that, David.'

She took the key gently from his fingers, stepped inside the room and started to close the door, still smiling, though her lips trembled slightly. 'I love you too. Goodnight.'

★　　★　　★

They got up the next morning to rain and freezing fog. David gave in to Simon's constant pestering to be on their way to visit Mendibel, though he would have preferred to wait until the weather improved. He admitted as much to Lorna, who shared his reservations, but then he took one look at Simon's distraught face and relented.

It was not going to be easy to negotiate the narrow, winding tracks that meandered in all directions through dense forests and wild mountainous landscapes; not to mention finding an isolated hamlet that had, reportedly, no more than a couple of dozen inhabitants.

'We'll go,' David said. 'But if the weather gets worse, no argument, we turn back. Is that clear, young man?'

Simon grinned and nodded, then ran off to collect his boots and waterproof.

The hotel owner's wife appeared with a basket filled with bread and cheese and a bottle of Txakoli, the local Basque wine.

Madame's husband pointed them in the right direction and told them to keep to the left on the high roads, when they would eventually reach Mendibel.

'Mais attention, mes amis!' he said, holding on to the car door. 'The people here are very private. They do not like questions, so you must not be surprised if they treat you like spies. Spies they had in number during the war, you understand.'

'They will not trust you easily, so be warned.'

★   ★   ★

'Do you think he was serious?' Lorna said. 'About the people being unfriendly?'

'Most likely,' David replied. 'Much the same thing happens in the English country villages, and they're not nearly so isolated as the villages here in France.'

Lorna gave a shudder and pulled her

coat closer about her, burying her hands in its deep pockets.

'Something to look forward to,' she muttered, then settled back to watch the road and kilometre after kilometre of trees standing sentry-like, marking their route.

'How long will it take?' Simon asked, unable to contain his excitement now that they were finally on their way to the place where Max's plane had come down more than a decade ago.

'It will take what it takes,' David said tersely, as he wrestled with the steering wheel on a particularly slippery slope.

'That's if we get there at all.'

Lorna was clinging on to the sides of her seat for dear life, too scared to say anything, but determined to show courage in front of her son. She looked out of the window and wished she hadn't. There was a sheer drop and the wheels were dangerously close to the edge. She gulped and closed her eyes, putting her trust in David's driving, which had been excellent all the way.

'Keep an eye open for oncoming vehicles, Lorna.'

Through her fear she heard David's instruction and her eyes snapped open. They were, of course, driving an English car and the French normally drove on the other side of the road. However, this road only seemed wide enough for one car, so if anything were coming the other way, it would be a disaster. Even on wider roads, the French tended to drive in the middle, giving the deep ditches on either side a wide berth.

'Oh, dear!' No sooner had the thought of unexpected oncoming traffic entered her head, than a farm tractor rounded the corner directly ahead of them.

David jammed on his brakes, almost tumbling Lorna and Simon from their seats. Tyres squealed as the car sent grit and stones over the edge, where they went bouncing down a near vertical slope to the road far below.

'Blast!' David banged several times

on his horn, whether from fear, anger or frustration, it wasn't clear.

'Wow!' Simon exclaimed, scrambling back on to his seat and bracing his feet against the back of Lorna's seat. He had been scared for a moment, but the fear had passed and he was now enjoying the moment of drama.

The tractor stopped in front of them with inches to spare and the driver sat scratching his head and regarding the foreign car and its occupants from on high.

'What do we do now?' Lorna couldn't keep the quiver out of her voice.

'Just stay put, you two,' David said, getting out of the car and walking gingerly along the edge of the track towards the tractor driver.

Lorna watched him speaking to the fellow, his arms going like windmills as he did his best to explain the difficulties, and to understand the response. The big Basque kept shrugging, and then he finally got down from the tractor and marched in front of

54

David to the car, climbing in behind the wheel without hesitation. He spent a few seconds being a little dumbfounded by the right-hand drive, then found reverse gear and shot the car back at breathtaking speed.

'Wow!' was all Simon could say, as he ducked down behind the front passenger seat.

Lorna was too frightened to do anything but hold her breath until they came to a stop, completely off the road and leaning at an unbelievable forty-five degree angle.

The Frenchman then nodded to Lorna and touched a grubby, work-worn finger to the edge of his big black beret. He got out, leaving the car's engine purring, and returned to his tractor, which he proceeded to drive past them without giving them a further glance.

'Don't move!' David was getting carefully behind the wheel and hauling on the handbrake to stop the car rolling away from its precarious position.

'I don't think I'll ever be able to move again,' Lorna whispered, her eyes staring straight ahead. She heard a nervous giggle from behind. Simon would no doubt deny it, but she was silently betting that his legs were as jelly-like as her own.

★ ★ ★

They were soon back on track and proceeding slowly around the next bend. Fortunately, there were no rogue tractors waiting to frighten them a second time, so they all breathed sighs of relief, then burst out laughing.

It had been frightening for a while, but it had succeeded in jolting them into a better frame of mind. And even the sun decided to show a pale face and burn off some of the fog that was still hanging around.

They picnicked at midday in a clearing, with felled trees for seats and a flat rock for a table. Simon was allowed a taste of the wine, but wasn't impressed.

'Ugh! It's like medicine,' he said, diving into the picnic basket and finding an orange instead.

Lorna took a sip from her glass and grimaced as the sharp white wine hit the back of her throat and made her eyes sting.

'He's right,' she told David, who was laughing at both of them. 'I think you could remove paint with this.'

'It's the tannin from the grapes they use,' he said, savouring his wine delicately like a connoisseur, allowing the flavour to roll around his palate. 'This isn't too bad, actually. It's young, but I get a definite flavour of green grapes. It might be better for being put down for a year or two.'

'Put down the sink, do you mean?' Simon grinned cheekily and David made a half-hearted swipe at him with a baguette.

'You have a lot of growing up to do, my boy!'

'But not too fast, eh?' Lorna said, as Simon ran off to explore. She gazed wistfully after him. 'Sometimes I think he's already stopped being a child. It makes me so sad.'

David patted her knee and handed her a chunk of bread and some thick pâté. 'You can't keep him a child forever, Lorna.'

'I know,' she said, 'but I keep thinking how much Max has missed, not seeing his son. Not being there for him when Simon needed a father figure. Sometimes I'm afraid for Simon. This fixation he's got, insisting that Max is still alive. It's not exactly healthy, is it?'

'Perhaps this trip will put an end to all his crazy dreams.' David fixed her with a piercing gaze. 'Lorna, when we get back to England, I think we should make plans to get married.'

Lorna felt a frown creasing her forehead. A happy smile right now would have been nice, but she couldn't manage it. Suddenly, the happy-ever-after future with David was crowding in a little too closely.

She liked the idea of it, felt the need to settle down to a normal family life, but she couldn't quite get beyond the thought. Every time she tried, it was as if a heavy door slammed shut in her mind, leaving her on one side of it and David on the other.

'Let's talk about that later, shall we?' she said. 'This isn't the right time.'

'Will there ever be a right time, Lorna?'

'Yes, of course,' she said, the heat of her denial, or was it her guilt, glowing red in her cheeks. 'It's just . . . well, I don't know, David, I can't even explain it to myself. Being here, knowing that Max might be not too far away from where we are right now . . . '

'You feel as if you're being unfaithful to him,' David finished for her, and she nodded. 'I thought as much.'

'I know it's not fair to keep you hanging on,' she said, her eyes searching the forest that rose steeply, sweeping up to the distant, snow-covered peaks that were getting ever closer. 'I'm sorry.'

'Don't, for goodness sake, tell me that you don't deserve me,' David said with a short, mirthless laugh.

'No, I won't do that,' Lorna said. 'But I will make you a promise. Once this trip is over, I'll give you my decision, one way or the other.'

'No more waiting?'

'No more waiting.'

'Promise?'

She hesitated, hearing her son's footsteps approaching down the one visible track through the trees. 'I promise.'

★   ★   ★

'Hey, Mum! David!' Simon crashed through the bushes beside them, rosy-cheeked and breathing hard. 'There's a valley on the other side of this hill and I saw smoke rising. Do you think it's Mendibel?'

'It might very well be,' David said.

'Well, come on!' Simon shouted. 'Let's go.'

And he was off again, running up the

hill, dodging bushes and trees, as sprightly as a young deer. He had disappeared over the next ridge before they had time to gather up their things and follow in his wake.

'Oh, dear!' Lorna gasped breathlessly, glancing anxiously at the spot where he had disappeared.

'What's wrong?' David asked.

'Nothing. I'm all right, really I am,' she said, forcing a smile. 'I don't know why I said that, really.'

'Never mind. Hop into the car and we'll pick Simon up further along the track.'

And then she said it again, but this time to herself, 'Oh, dear!'

What lay over the next hill, she wondered? Inhospitable people. A relic of a long-lost aircraft. Shattered dreams.

Simon Finds An Ally

Simon was waiting for them at the top of a track that dropped steeply into a tiny valley that formed a natural amphitheatre. He pointed to the small cluster of buildings huddled at the heart of it. Burbling brooks and mountain streams made silvery trails through its centre.

'Well, it looks as if you were right, Simon. Unless I'm very much mistaken, this must be Mendibel,' David said.

Lorna stared down at the hamlet with its blue-grey slate roofs. Curling columns of wood smoke rose from the squat chimneys, mingling with the misty wraiths that rose from the warmed earth. Faint sounds echoed eerily through the silence that surrounded them. It was a silence that could only be created by the enveloping arms of a dense forest.

Then, as if taking their cues from the arrival of the small group, a cockerel crowed, a dog barked and a clock chimed the hour. Someone, somewhere, was sawing wood and there was a muffled cackle of geese, punctuated by the raucous quacking of ducks splashing about in a pond.

'It's magical,' Lorna breathed. 'You'd think we'd just stepped back in time.'

David came to stand beside her, draping an arm affectionately about her shoulders. It felt good and solid and real in this strangely mysterious place.

'At a guess, the place hasn't seen many changes for centuries,' he said. 'No telephone, and probably no wireless. I doubt they've even heard of television. It's no wonder they're suspicious of strangers.'

'Did you say that you have the name of the man who found the tail fin from Max's plane?' Lorna asked.

'Yes. Roberto Lafon. He's the mayor, among other things, which includes being a cheese-maker, a wine-maker and, when necessary, a mountain rescue guide. He was with a group of botanists when they found it.'

There was the sound of steam hissing, which proved to be Simon, who had been pacing up and down, looking longingly at the nestling hamlet. 'Why are we standing here? Come on!'

He started walking until David called him back and ordered him into the car.

'We'll do this properly,' David said. 'If we barge into the village with all guns blazing they might decide to clam up and tell us nothing. You heard what *monsieur* at the hotel said. They don't like strangers. And they probably like strangers even less when they're foreign and asking questions.'

'Did you hear that, Simon?' Lorna climbed into the front passenger seat and hoped that her son wasn't going to choose this moment to become difficult. 'David's right. If we upset these people they may never help us, so let's tread carefully, shall we?'

Simon gave her a sulky glare, but settled down and didn't utter another word while David manoeuvred the car carefully down the track.

After a lot of bumping and rising of dust clouds, they came to a cobbled square encircled by the most rustic buildings Lorna had ever seen.

'Would you believe,' David said, nodding towards the most ramshackle building directly in front of them, 'that there's a *bar*?'

Lorna gave an amused laugh. 'Well, that's probably the best place to ask about the mayor,' she said.

'They have a mayor in a village?' Simon leaned over the back of Lorna's seat and squinted through the dusty windscreen. 'Wow!'

'It's not like England,' David explained, 'where you only have mayors in towns and cities. In France, every community, large and small, has its own mayor. It's looked upon as a very important role. They are powerful people, so watch your manners, young sir, or you might get sent to the guillotine.'

At that, Simon laughed, and then he looked wary.

'They don't have guillotines in France any more, do they?'

'Who knows,' David teased. 'Besides, this is Basque country and they're a law unto themselves.'

'Don't worry,' Simon nodded gravely. 'I'll be good.'

'I'm glad to hear it,' David said. 'Now out you both get. I don't know about anybody else, but I'm ready for a beer after that dusty ride.'

Lorna looked back to the track they had just descended and found it still hazy with dust despite the rain that had fallen earlier that day. It swirled about like blurred phantom shapes. She shivered, then turned to follow David and Simon into the old-fashioned *bar-tabac*. Which was when she noticed a young woman observing her from the doorway of a nearby house.

The girl was dark in a pretty,

intensely foreign way. She wore a shawl, like many of the countrywomen they had seen on the way, and her skirt was long and flowing, reaching almost to her slim ankles. Under her arm she carried a wicker basket full of laundry. But it was the expression in her eyes that struck Lorna. It was more than suspicious. There was a distinct flash of open resentment.

'How ridiculous,' she thought. 'Am I being paranoid, or does she already dislike me before we've actually met?'

'Bonjour mademoiselle!' Lorna smiled and nodded encouragingly, but the girl's expression did not change. Nor did she reply, but simply tossed her head in a haughty fashion and walked off down a narrow alleyway between the houses.

★ ★ ★

David had already ordered a beer for himself, coffee for Lorna and lemonade for Simon. He carried the drinks to a small round table by an open chimney that was big enough to roast an ox in. The rheumy-eyed barman watched them with unbridled curiosity.

'I've asked about Roberto Lafon,' David said. 'The barman's sent his lad out to fetch him. Apparently, our Monsieur Lafon is also the local teacher. He's certainly a man of many talents. It wouldn't surprise me in the least to find that he's the doctor and the dentist, as well.'

His attempt at introducing some light-hearted banter into the situation came to an abrupt halt when the young Frenchwoman reappeared. Looking more like a Spanish flamenco dancer than a simple French countrywoman, she was silhouetted in the bar doorway. One hand was above her head, supporting her weight on the doorjamb, while the other rested on a shapely hip. Lorna didn't know why the girl or her insolent pose should affect her, but it did. There was something oddly threatening about her, as she stood there silently surveying them through narrowed eyes.

'Good grief!' David breathed out the words as the girl stepped inside and crossed the floor in front of them, her skirt whirling about her calves. 'I think the cabaret has just arrived.'

'I doubt she has music or dancing in her heart,' Lorna said, giving Simon a warning nudge because he was sniggering, red-faced, into his lemonade. 'I saw her earlier. She doesn't seem too friendly.'

The barman looked up as he refilled a glass of frothing beer. Without a word he nodded to the girl, and then inclined his head in the direction of the English threesome huddled by the crackling log fire. She moved slowly toward them and stood frowning at them.

'I am Carla, wife of *Monsieur Lafon*, mayor of this commune,' she said in halting English.

'Hello!' Simon said.

'Ah, *bonjour, Madame Lafon!*' Ever the gentleman, David extended his hand in greeting. The young woman simply gave a haughty toss of her proud head.

69

'You will come with me to the schoolhouse,' she said, already heading for the door and stepping outside. 'My husband is there. He will speak to you, but he is . . . how you say? *Très occupé*, Very busy.'

'In that case, it's very kind of Monsieur Lafon to see us,' David said. 'We'll try not to take up too much of his time.'

He motioned to Lorna and Simon to follow as he went in the wake of the strange, unsmiling Frenchwoman, who was already striding out of the *bar-tabac* and making her way swiftly across the square.

* * *

The schoolhouse was a large room at the back of the house where Lorna had first seen Carla Lafon. It opened out on to a rectangle of balding grass, which the children obviously used as a playground.

There were a variety of items strewn

70

about and a handful of young children and a tangle-haired dog chasing a deflated rugby ball.

The mayor's wife snapped out a command to the children, who all jumped to attention before running off.

'*Entrez, entrez!*' A male voice sailed through the open window, and then a smiling face appeared. He beckoned to them and they entered the room. 'Welcome! I am Roberto Lafon. I am told you want my assistance. Is that not so?'

He was a pleasant-looking man, considerably older than his wife. As he spoke, he gave them a cursory glance, dark eyes twinkling through thick spectacles. He immediately went on with the business of wiping the lesson for the day from the blackboard. Despite his age, which had to be bordering on fifty, he had an athletic build and looked tremendously fit. It was not hard to imagine that his outdoor pursuits outweighed the time spent in the village, either as mayor or schoolmaster.

'Is it true that you found a piece of a plane, *monsieur*?' David said, having decided that they had exchanged sufficient pleasantries and it was time to get down to business.

'In the forest, yes.' Roberto Lafon wiped the chalk dust from his hands and perched on the edge of a desk. 'But I no longer have this. It was taken away by the British government. Why does it interest you?'

'My husband was on that plane, Monsieur Lafon,' Lorna said, pushing Simon in front of her. 'This is our son. Simon never knew his father, but he believes that there is a chance that Max could still be alive.'

The Frenchman's eyes, which had been brittle and inquisitive, sharpened, then softened as they left her face and transferred to that of the child before him.

'Ah, I see.'

'Is he still alive?' Simon asked eagerly. 'Do you know him?'

'And the name of your father?'

'Max!' Simon almost shouted out the name, then looked plaintively at his mother.

'My husband was Captain Maxwell Barrett,' Lorna said.

'He played the violin,' Simon supplied. 'Everybody knew him. He was famous.'

Monsieur Lafon regarded the boy again, head on one side. He then switched his attention to his wife, who was hovering in the open doorway. There was a rapid exchange of words between husband and wife in their own Basque language. Lorna saw the girl give a start, heard her gasp, saw the way her hand found its way to her throat, as if what her husband had told her was shocking. She shook her head vehemently.

'There are no Englishmen here,' she said in a low, barely audible voice. 'The war has ended long ago. Besides, we do not welcome foreigners.'

'Carla!' It was a short, sharp reproof from her husband. 'Perhaps you could bring us some tea, eh?'

When she scowled at him, but went to do his bidding, he smiled at them all apologetically. 'Sometimes, my wife is overcome by her passionate nature. She does not remember the war with fond memories.'

'None of us do,' David said.

'Ah, but *monsieur*, Carla was a victim of that war, more than most. You must forgive her if she seems a little . . . cold.'

'Do you have children, *monsieur*?' Lorna asked, feeling the need to draw the conversation away from the French girl and back on track. She could see that Simon was fidgeting and bursting to obtain information from the teacher about his find in the forest.

'Alas, no.' Monsieur Lafon hesitated, then: 'My wife has a child. He was the eldest of the children you saw earlier.'

'Your wife looks too young to have children of any age,' David said, showing his surprise at the news.

The Frenchman nodded slowly and

studied his hands as if they held some vast secret. 'She was only sixteen when she gave birth to Mixel,' he said eventually. 'We do not speak of it.'

There was a long, uncomfortable silence when nobody seemed to know what to say. They spent some time inspecting the classroom, talking about education, and then the rattle of a tray announced Carla's return with the tea.

'We wondered,' Lorna said to Roberto Lafon, 'if you would be kind enough to show us where you found the piece of tail fin, and, if possible, where you think the plane might have crashed.'

Out of the corner of her eye she saw Carla stiffen. 'You think my husband has nothing better to do than look for something that does not exist?' Anger resonated in her voice.

'Of course not, but . . . ' Lorna could not believe the intensity of the Frenchwoman's animosity.

'We'll pay you for your time, of course,' David said hastily. 'It's very important — for the boy, you see.'

Roberto spread his hands and gave a shrug.

'I do not mind giving the time,' he said. 'The children are now on holiday for Christmas.'

'Roberto, no!' His wife had jumped to her feet.

'Enough, Carla! The extra money will be good for the children. We will buy books for the school. Next month I will take you to Biarritz and buy them and pens and pencils and slates on which they can do their lessons.'

But she wasn't listening. She was already flouncing out of the room. They heard the whisper of her slippered feet on the stone tiles and the slamming of a door, and then silence reigned once more.

'Does that mean you'll take us, sir?' Simon said, full of enthusiasm, oblivious to the young woman's angry outburst.

'Simon, we can't force Monsieur Lafon to do what we want,' Lorna said, touching her son's shoulder with a placating hand. 'Not if it's going to cause trouble between him and his wife . . . '

'Take no notice of Carla,' Roberto said. 'It is her Spanish blood overheating, that is all. Her father was a Spanish Basque. He died before she was born. Her mother was from this commune, but, alas, she also is dead.'

'How sad,' Lorna said.

'Monsieur Lafon . . . ?' Simon began, but the Frenchman held up a staying hand.

'I can see, young *monsieur*, that all this . . . this voyage of discovery, shall we say . . . it is all for you.' Lafon smoothed a finger over his black moustache, his eyes twinkling. 'What makes you so sure that your father is still alive?' he asked.

'He is, I know he is!'

'But what evidence have you to persuade me to give up my valuable time to look for this mythical English gentleman?'

'He's not mythical!' Simon objected, ignoring his mother's warning glance. 'Mythical people aren't real. They're just in fairytales. My father . . . '

'Your father, Simon, was in a plane that lost its way. It must have run out of fuel and crashed somewhere in this vast countryside.'

'Listen to Monsieur Lafon, Simon,' David said, trying hard not to sound biased, but Lorna knew whose side he was on.

'I *am* listening, but . . . ' Simon's voice was full of emotion. 'I know all about that bandleader . . . you know . . . Glenn Miller. He was an American and his plane crashed in the English Channel and they never found him, but *he's* dead.'

Monsieur Lafon nodded sagely. 'And the world lost a great musician. Just like your father.'

'But that's just it!' Simon's resolve showed no sign of weakening. 'My father isn't dead!'

'What makes you so sure?' Lafon

persevered calmly.

Simon hung his head for a moment, then his chin came up and he fixed the Frenchman with an unwavering eye.

'I feel it in here.' He slapped his chest, his hands landing with a dull thud over his heart. 'Please, Monsieur Lafon . . . please help me to find my father!'

The Frenchman gave a long, low sigh. 'Simon,' he said, 'if I am to be your guide, you must call me Roberto, yes?'

'Yes!' Simon shouted.

Lorna and David looked on helplessly. Each of them was wondering how things would be in the end, when Monsieur Lafon would be obliged to stop searching, and Simon had to finally accept the truth; that his father was, indeed, dead.

A Dream Dashed

'Are you sure you're going to be all right, you two, if I leave you here on your own?' David asked, as he prepared to return to St Jean Pied de Port, from where he hoped to get in some skiing. 'It seems very selfish.'

'Don't feel guilty, David,' Lorna told him, knowing how disappointed he was at missing his holiday in Switzerland. 'Roberto's mother has given us a very nice room in her house. We'll be fine.'

'Yes, Roberto seems to be a good sport. I'm sure you'll be in good hands.'

'Simon already thinks he's something of a hero,' Lorna laughed, and then pulled a face. 'I can't say the same about Carla Lafon, though. She's a bit of a dragon, isn't she?'

'A young and pretty dragon,' David said. 'And she probably sees you as competition. In case you haven't noticed, there aren't many young men around here, and the older ones aren't exactly the stuff that romantic dreams are made of.'

'That's true,' Lorna laughed. 'But she has nothing to fear from me, I can assure you.'

'Maybe it's Carla you need to reassure.' David grinned boyishly and tapped a finger under her chin. 'After all, you will be tramping through the forest with her husband and he already has a twinkle in his eye when he looks at you.'

'Well, he can just un-twinkle,' Lorna said firmly, standing on tiptoe to plant a kiss on David's cheek.

'You'd better be off before the light fades. I don't like to think of you driving on these mountain roads in the dark. Especially if there are any tractors lurking.'

'Oh, don't remind me! I thought we were going to go over the edge!'

David slid behind the wheel of his car

and started the engine. As Lorna shut the door for him, he took her hand and gave it an affectionate squeeze.

'Are you sure you're going to be all right, darling?' he said. 'If you'd prefer me to stay, just tell me.'

'Of course we'll be all right!' Why did she feel less certain than she sounded? 'Off you go and enjoy your skiing.'

She knew that David would only get bored and twitchy if he stayed. Taking part in a futile search, knowing that it would all end in tears, would only make him irritable, and that irritation might be directed at Simon. Her poor son had enough to contend with without that, and it might just turn him more and more against the man who was hoping to be his stepfather.

'I'll be back in a couple of days to check on you,' David said, squeezing her hand more firmly. 'Simon might have had enough of the forest by then and be longing to get back home to England.'

'Anything's possible,' Lorna said, and bent to kiss him on the lips. 'I'm sure that once he gets this thing about Max out of his head, he'll settle down and we can become a proper family.'

'Yes, I'm sure you're right,' David said, but he didn't look too convinced. He wound up his window and drove off.

Lorna watched the dust trail as he made his way up the rough clay track. The glass and chrome on the car glinted in a sun that was already pink-tinged as it dropped slowly behind the mountains.

When the car's red tail-lights finally blinked out of sight, she experienced a yawning emptiness inside her. Giving an involuntary shudder, she wrapped her arms about herself and hurried back into the house, where she was greeted warmly by old Madame Lafon's ageing Pyrenean mountain dog. At least, she thought, the animals were friendly.

'He's super, isn't he?' Simon knelt down in front of the dog and buried his hands in its dense coat. 'Do you think I could have a dog like this one day, Mum?'

Lorna smiled down on him. 'It's a big responsibility taking on a dog, Simon. They need looking after, lots of exercise . . . '

'I could do that!'

'You have to go to school,' she reminded him. 'And I have my job at the library. The poor animal would be alone for hours on end.'

'But you don't have to work,' Simon said, scrunching up his face as the big dog licked the inside of his ear with its pink tongue.

'No, but I want to,' she said, thinking how her job had helped keep her sane over the past few years. 'Come on, Simon. Let's unpack our cases and prepare our clothes for tomorrow. Remember, you must wear something warm and take extra socks. We can't have you catching cold.'

He immediately gave up the petting of the dog, and she knew that tomorrow's search would be uppermost in his mind. No doubt he would have trouble getting to sleep that night because of his excitement. And Lorna thought that he would not be the only one, though excitement wasn't exactly what was nagging at her.

Her thoughts had been confused from the moment they had arrived and she was trying her hardest not to think at all.

★   ★   ★

After a night of disturbed sleep, listening to the sounds of the ancient house, which included the snoring of Roberto's mother, Lorna was glad when it was time to get up. She could have done without the loud banging on the bedroom door from old Madame Lafon, however. The woman spoke not a word of English and muttered all the time in a mixture of Basque and French with a heavy, guttural accent. The muttering accompanied her every move, and she seemed oblivious to the fact that her visitors did not understand.

Lorna found her voice after the second assault on the door panel. She could hear Simon making reluctant sounds from the depths of his covers, after a night tossing and turning.

'*Merci, madame!*' she called out.

Lorna sat up in bed and pulled the quilt up to her chin as the elderly Frenchwoman threw open the door and marched in, bearing a breakfast tray. There was the traditional bowl of *café au lait* for Lorna and one of milk for Simon, but this time there was goat's cheese as well as homemade plum preserve with chunks of crusty black bread.

Madame Lafon pointed a crooked finger at the food on the tray. She also pointed to the jug of cold water and the wide bowl in which it sat. Lorna smiled, nodded and thanked her. She hadn't expected breakfast in bed.

Madame Lafon gave a grunt and went back down the creaking staircase to the kitchen below, where she slept on a pull-down bed. Roberto had assured Lorna that this had been her choice for twenty years. His mother was not, therefore, giving up her bedroom for the unforeseen guests.

'Come on, sleepyhead!' She went to the small cot that Simon was occupying and shook his shoulder until he stirred and groaned and showed two sleep-filled eyes over the quilt. 'We have a real treat,' Lorna told him.

'What is it?' Simon was sitting up, but his eyes were still half shut. 'Bacon and eggs?'

'If only!' Lorna dipped her fingertips in the icy water and flicked a few drops in her son's flushed face.

'Argh! What's that?'

'It's all we have to get washed in,' she told him brightly. 'Just for once, though, you can have your breakfast before you wash. At least the coffee and the milk's hot.'

A few minutes later, after the quickest wash he had ever managed, Simon stood before Lorna, fully dressed and raring to go.

'Aren't you ready yet?' he wanted to know.

'Give me a minute,' she told him, gulping down the last mouthful of her coffee.

'Come on! Roberto's probably already waiting for us.'

'I don't think there's the remotest chance that he'll go without us,' Lorna chastised gently. 'Now, how many layers have you got on under that jacket? It's going to be very cold out there in the forest.'

'I've got on a vest and two jerseys,' Simon informed her, dodging away from her enquiring fingers.

'Is that your new jumper I can see?'

He looked apprehensive. 'You won't make me take it off, will you, Mum? It's blue. It's my father's favourite colour. You told me so.'

'Yes, I did, but . . . '

'Please don't make me take it off.'

She gave a smile and touched his

cheek. It was important to stay positive, for his sake. He would be disillusioned soon enough.

'Of course you can keep it on,' she said brightly. 'It's the warmest jumper you've got.'

She started to reach for her outdoor things and found that he was there before her, helping her on with her boots and her coat, his child's hands clumsy in their haste.

By the time they got downstairs, Madame Lafon was feeding the chickens at the back of the house. The birds clucked noisily around her feet as she threw them handfuls of corn.

She took little notice of Lorna and Simon as they emerged into the hazy sunshine, but straightened her back stiffly and issued a strident call over the dividing wall between her house and the schoolhouse.

There was a cheery response and two minutes later, Roberto Lafon appeared, well equipped for a day in the forest.

'Ah, I am glad to see that you are

warmly dressed, and with good shoes.' He greeted them with a firm handshake. 'At this time of year the forest is cold and damp, even when the sun shines.'

There followed a brief exchange of small talk, and then they set off, following a narrow trail that led up into the foothills. Like a terrier, anxious to reach his destination, Simon kept running on ahead, then doubling back to check that he was going in the right direction.

★   ★   ★

'I'm so grateful to you for this,' Lorna told Roberto, when they stopped to catch their breath after the first steep climb.

Roberto shrugged and stared past her into the distance where the sun was giving rise to ghostly patches of steam as it warmed up the damp leaves and undergrowth.

All around them was the sound of

water dripping and the odd rustle of snakes and lizards and other forest creatures searching for the first food of the day.

'What makes the boy believe so strongly that his father is alive?' Roberto had picked up a stone and was studying it closely, turning it over and over in his hand, his fingertips tracing the cream and beige lines sandwiched between pink and grey. Stones like this were to be found everywhere in the region.

'I don't know.' Lorna eased the straps of her canvas backpack, thinking that she would be glad when they stopped for lunch and lightened the load by eating the food Madame Lafon had provided for them.

'And you? Do you believe that you will find him?'

Lorna started to shake her head, then decided that she did not want to sound so negative.

'What I would like and what I believe is possible are two separate things,' she said. 'It's hardly likely that Max could still be alive, but we need closure. Me, Simon . . . and David.'

'Ah, yes, David.' Roberto threw down the stone, but still had a contemplative look in his dark eyes. 'He's in love with you, non?'

'We are very close . . . yes.' She explained briefly how well the three of them had been getting along until the papers had reported the recent find of the tail section from Max's plane. 'Until then I thought I was over losing my husband. I was ready to commit myself to a new life with David.'

'Ah.' Roberto inclined his head. 'I see.'

'Everything seemed fine,' Lorna told him. 'The future suddenly looked brighter. The pain . . . the real pain of grief . . . had gone. Or, at least, lessened.'

'And suddenly, the past blew up in your face and your son began to believe in miracles.' Roberto gave her a kindly look and she felt that he understood exactly how she was feeling. 'When you love deeply, as you obviously loved your husband, it is easy to believe in miracles. I still believe, sometimes, that I will turn a corner and find my wife standing there, smiling, arms outstretched.'

'I'm sorry, I didn't know . . .'

'How could you? She died many years ago, giving birth to our first child.'

He pushed back a lank strand of dark hair that had fallen over his forehead and smiled. 'Shall we continue? I see that Simon has already disappeared over the next ridge.'

They stopped at midday and ate a hearty lunch of bread and pâté and goat's cheese, by which time the temperature had risen and was comfortable for walking.

Lorna tried not to be too single-minded about their expedition. The forests were abundant in wildlife and she enjoyed the sights and sounds of the small animals, the insects and the birds, thinking how Max would have appreciated them, too, if only he had been there with them.

'In the springtime, and in summer,' Roberto told her, as he gathered wild mushrooms from the mossy earth beneath the trees, 'there are butterflies and flowers. The air is perfumed with pine and wild thyme. There is not this earthy, musky scent that we have in winter. You must come back in summer.'

Lorna smiled, but did not say anything. Somehow, she didn't think that she would want to return. No, she must try to get Simon to accept that his father was lost to them forever. It wasn't fair to David to keep Max's memory alive, as if he were still a part of them, in flesh and blood. It would be sufficient, she thought, to hold him in their hearts, quietly, privately. Her memories of her time with Max would certainly never fade. They would always be there, waiting to be revisited and savoured when the moment was right.

★ ★ ★

'There's a red flag!' They heard Simon's excited shout before they saw the top of his head appear over the rise ahead. Then he was running down the incline towards them, oblivious of fallen twigs, branches and stones, which his hasty feet dislodged.

The flag had been placed there by Roberto the day the piece of wreckage had been found, to mark the spot where it lay. That piece of Max's plane had since been removed and identified, but it was the only remnant of the fated plane to turn up, despite thorough searching at the time.

'But surely,' Lorna said, her heart flipping as she looked upon the flag, 'if it fell here, the plane can't be far away.'

She looked all round them, willing something to jump out at her, but all she could see were banks of trees rising up to summits of the mountains on one side and running down to the sea on the other.

Roberto frowned at the soft, fern-tangled earth at their feet. 'There was a storm that night. They lost contact with the plane. It is possible that they were blown off-course. They may even have been going in the wrong direction. We don't know.'

'So the plane could have come down in the sea?'

'That is one possibility, yes.'

'But how do you explain that bit of tail fin being found here?'

Roberto looked thoughtful, standing there, his shoulders hunched, his chin on his chest.

'It had sheered off,' he said. 'Perhaps they hit a tree — but kept going until they fell into the sea. Or they could have come down in one of the deep crevasses. People have been disappearing in these mountains as long as man has walked the earth.'

'But what if the plane came down here, in the forest?' It was Simon who put the anxious question.

'Then we would have found it, *petit*.' Roberto shaded his eyes as dappled sunlight fell through the canopy above them. 'Whether it came down in the sea or in a crevasse in the higher mountains, it makes no difference. Either way, there would be no survivors.'

'Unless they had parachutes.'

Roberto smiled and patted the boy's shoulder. 'They may not have had time to jump before the plane crashed. No, Simon, I'm afraid your father, together with the others on his plane, are no longer with us.'

'Can we look a bit farther?' Simon said, reluctant to accept so soon what the Frenchman was saying. 'The forest goes on for miles, and then there's the mountains, and . . .'

'Simon, please . . .' Lorna saw her son's face quiver and crumple and his eyes fill with tears.

'Oh, Mum, we can't give up yet!'

'Sweetheart, Monsieur Lafon is an expert. He knows the forest and the mountains. If he says there is no chance of finding your father or his plane, then we have to believe him.'

Simon looked at her, his face awash

with tears. He pulled away when she tried to comfort him.

'You don't *want* to find him, do you? You want to go back to England and marry David.'

Lorna glanced at Roberto, who was standing apart from them, leaving them some private space.

'Simon, you're still too young to understand, but I'll tell you anyway. I would give anything to have your father back with us, alive and well. But we can't always have what we want. We have to move on, to live as best we can. Your father would be the first person to understand that. He loved life and he would hate for either of us to waste what precious time we have running after a dream that can never come true.'

'Monsieur Lafon?' Simon called out to Roberto with a pleading look.

'Your mother is right,' Roberto said. 'Come. We must go back. It is not good to be caught in these forests when darkness falls and it is forecast for bad weather tonight.'

Simon's narrow chest rose and fell with his uneven, urgent breathing. There was an audible sob that tore at his throat and his lips quivered. He said no more, but spun around on his heel and marched back down the hill in front of them, his shoulders slumped despondently.

*　*　*

'I am sorry,' Roberto said, helping Lorna down a particularly steep slope. 'I should have refused to bring you.'

'You've been very kind,' Lorna said. 'When Simon has had time to calm down, I'm sure he'll accept the facts. He's not a stupid boy, which is why I can't understand this behaviour he's adopted lately.'

'He is a good boy,' Roberto said.

'Yes, I think his father would have been very proud of him.'

'Tell me, Lorna,' Roberto said, turning his bright, intelligent gaze on her to watch her face when she answered him. 'You have not accepted your husband's death yet, either, have you?'

'No,' she said after a long pause. 'I can't explain it, Roberto. Not even to myself. But there's never been the feeling that Max has gone completely. That's the hardest thing I've had to cope with in my life. My head tells me he's dead, but my heart can still feel him reaching out to me, touching me.'

Roberto fell silent for the rest of the journey, except when he was required to confirm which track to follow. He seemed to be deep in thought and his eyes looked troubled. Lorna, too, felt the weight of an unknown sadness and hoped that David would be back tomorrow as he had promised, and they could all go off skiing together. Anything to take their minds off the subject of the crashed plane, and Max.

Once he got the feel of his skis and all that snow, Simon would surely cheer up. He couldn't go on forever searching for a man he had never met, even if that man was his father.

Tomorrow, she would have another long talk with her son. Tomorrow, everything would seem better, clearer.

Wouldn't it?

Carla Acts Strangely

They had returned to the village by the most direct route, with Roberto keeping an anxious eye on the darkening sky. As predicted, long before their journey was at an end, storm clouds rolled in and great splotches of rain began to fall. They covered the last few hundred yards at a run. By the time they tumbled, breathlessly, through the door of Madame Lafon's house, they were soaked to the skin.

'*Vite, vite!*' Roberto's mother handed out towels in the hall and hurried back to the kitchen to stir the soup she was preparing for supper.

Above their heads thunder growled threateningly. The rain beat a heavy tattoo on the roof, and splattered like hot fat on the dry earth, scattering the poultry. The birds voiced their disapproval in no uncertain terms, squawking vociferously as they dashed for shelter.

Simon was doing his best not to sulk. Being moody was not a normal aspect of his usually pleasant personality. However, it was evident to Lorna that her son was hiding a heavy heart brought on by the day's disappointing search. It had turned out exactly as she had expected, but the one thing she was not going to do was say, I told you so. It was best to let Simon come to the truth by himself. No doubt, once he had had time to assimilate the facts, he would gradually let go of the idea that Max was still alive. Simon was tenacious, but he wasn't stupid.

'I'm not quite sure exactly what he expected out there today,' she said to Roberto, as they watched Simon trudge solemnly up the stairs to his room. 'Maybe he thought that he would find something that belonged to his father, but too many years have gone by. If there was anything, it's been buried long since.'

'He really does believe that his father

is still alive,' Roberto said, towelling his hair briskly so that it turned into shiny black curls. 'I find it curious that he is so . . . so confident.'

'Yes, I know,' Lorna sighed. 'How can you explain to an eleven-year-old that what he believes is an illusion?'

'That,' said Roberto, polishing his spectacles and replacing them on his long Gascon nose, 'is something I have never had to do. I do not envy you the task, Lorna.

'But I do envy you your son.'

There was a blip of silence between them. Lorna experienced a certain pang of pity for the Frenchman who hid so much sadness behind his twinkling eyes and genial smile.

'Well, David will be back tomorrow,' she said. 'Then we'll be gone and won't bother you or your family any more.'

'It is no bother!'

'I don't think your mother really wants us here, any more than your wife does.'

'My mother is glad of the company,'

Roberto said kindly. 'She is old and lonely and I, her only son, do not pay her enough attention. As for my wife . . . ' He blew out his lips in a typically French dismissive gesture. 'She is jealous, as well as suspicious of, strangers.'

He shook his head and gave a soft, mirthless laugh as he draped a waterproof over his head and turned for the door.

'Thank you for today, Roberto,' Lorna said, and he gave her a wide grin that took years off his age.

He must have been quite handsome as a young man, Lorna thought, but now the ravages of time and the outdoor life he led were engraving themselves on his features.

'It is my pleasure.' He hesitated, holding the door partly open and letting in a curtain of rain that made the old dog shift from its place with a grunt of disapproval. 'Your friend, David, will be happy. When it rains like this in the foothills, it brings much snow to the high mountains. The skiing will be good.'

'I hope he doesn't decide to stay on longer, in that case,' Lorna said.

'That is not a problem. Tomorrow, while you wait for him, bring Simon to the schoolhouse. He can meet the children. There are two boys near his age. It will be good for your son, and Mixel and his friend, Joseba, can practise their English.'

It sounded like a good idea, so she agreed to take Simon to meet the boys after breakfast the next day.

* * *

When she put it to Simon later, he greeted the news with mixed emotions. 'I was hoping we could go back into the forest.'

'Roberto says the weather is going to be bad for the next few days,' Lorna told him. 'Besides, David will be back soon and then he'll expect us to go skiing with him.'

'But I want to go back into the forest,' Simon insisted, a dark frown shadowing his face. 'I don't want to ski and I don't want to meet any boys.'

'Oh, come on, Simon.' Lorna tried to mask the fact that her patience was beginning to wear thin. 'You'll enjoy meeting the boys. It'll be fun. Think of all the questions you can ask them about the way they live. It's as good as a history lesson, because this place must be years behind its time.'

'I don't like history,' he said. 'It's my worst subject.'

'Well, here's a perfect chance for you to improve your knowledge. Talk to the boys and their parents. They must have lots of stories to tell you.'

Simon's chin shot up. Something she had said had ignited his enthusiasm.

'Yes! I could talk to the people in the village,' he said. 'You know, Mum . . . old people like Madame Lafon. Maybe some of them remember the plane coming down. They might be holding my father prisoner somewhere.'

'Goodness, Simon, what an imagination you have. There are no prisoners these days. In any case, the French were on our side.'

'Yes, I know, but . . . ' She saw a smile spread across his face. 'What did you say their names were?'

'The boys?' Oh, the relief to see interest in his face. 'They have unusual names. Basque, obviously. Mixel and Joseba.'

'Michael and Joseph.'

'Very likely,' Lorna said. 'Anyway, according to Roberto, they need to practise their English.'

'Great! I need to practise my French.'

He went to bed happily enough, and Lorna hoped that the business about his father would quickly fade, once the boys started doing what boys of their age enjoyed most, which was usually getting up to mischief.

★　★　★

The boys hit it off immediately, which was a great relief. Lorna didn't know why she should have entertained any doubts at all. Simon had Max's open, friendly personality that drew people to him, both young and old alike. And there was no problem with the language. Within half an hour, all three were chatting away in a mixture of English and French and looking as if they had known each other all their lives.

Roberto's young wife, Carla, had greeted them with a jaundiced eye and reluctantly invited them into her home. Minutes later, Roberto came downstairs, sleepy-eyed and yawning. However, he was the one to take charge of making coffee and warming croissants, despite Lorna's protest that she had already eaten breakfast at his mother's house an hour earlier.

'You cannot refuse the croissants of the great Roberto Lafon! I make them myself. Here, taste them. Are they not the best croissants you have ever had? And cream cheese from my goats. A little of that with my strawberry preserve and you will be in raptures.'

'Is there anything you can't do, Roberto?' Lorna said laughingly, then, after tasting the croissant with its unusual dressing, she had to agree that it was delicious.

All the time she was talking with Roberto and the boys were conversing companionably around the big family table, Carla Lafon held on to her brooding expression as she punished a pile of newly laundered clothes with a large flat iron. Every time she hung a still damp article over the rail around the fireplace she gave a surreptitious glance towards the table, and to Lorna in particular. Lorna tried not to notice, or be bothered by the girl's odd behaviour.

The rain had eased off somewhat, but as Roberto cleared away the dishes from the table, piling them noisily in the shallow, stoneware sink, blinding flashes of lightning crashed beyond the kitchen window. A deafening roar of thunder followed almost immediately.

Roberto stared morosely at the weather and gave a resigned shrug.

'I do not think David will be returning today,' he said. 'The roads will be flooded between St Jean Pied de Port and Mendibel. It would not be prudent to try.'

'Oh, but we can't possibly stay here any longer,' Lorna said, noticing another quick, even more piercing glance in her direction from Carla. 'It would be taking too much advantage of your mother's hospitality.'

'I will speak to my mother.' Roberto was already on his way to the door.

'Oh, no . . . please, Roberto . . . '

He silenced her with one finger raised.

'You have no choice,' he said. 'Besides, my mother has not yet had the opportunity of cooking her *specialité de la maison* for you. We cannot rob her of that pleasure.'

'Roberto!' The sharpness of Carla's voice left Lorna in no doubt that she was not in agreement with what her husband was suggesting. The rest of the conversation was conducted in rapid Basque. It seemed to Lorna that she was giving her husband a good tongue-lashing. Roberto stood firm and amazingly patient, though his eyes betrayed his irritation.

'No, Carla, *mon amour.*' Roberto had the final word, dismissing his wife with an admonishing shake of the head.

He turned then and smiled at Lorna reassuringly. 'She is concerned for the state of the roads, but I am sure that David is wise enough to stay where he is until the weather improves.'

Why did Lorna feel that he was lying to her? What reason would he have for not telling her the truth of what his wife's concerns really were? It was a mystery to her, and one she thought she might never get to the bottom of. It was also just one of the many reasons why she would be glad to leave Mendibel and turn her back firmly on everything here in the Iraty forest.

★　★　★

Roberto left them without a further word. Carla, keeping her face averted and fixed with a stony expression, picked up a pile of neatly ironed clothes and flounced upstairs.

At the table, Simon was too involved with exchanging information with his two new Basque friends to notice. He was smiling, Lorna observed thankfully. Curiously, she edged her way closer to the small group of children, intrigued to hear how well they were communicating in each other's language.

'And you think he will know where my father is?' Simon was saying, as she approached.

'Yes, I am sure he will know,' the older boy called Mixel said, nodding his head like a wise old man. 'Olentzero knows everything.'

Oh, no, Lorna thought. Simon just can't let the matter drop.

She drew in a deep breath, squared her shoulders and leaned on the table.

Suddenly aware of her presence, three young heads turned in her direction.

'Who is this Olentzero?' she said, feeling that she might as well enter into the spirit of the discussion rather than fall out with her son. 'Does he live here in Mendibel?'

Mixel shook his head and the younger boy, Joseba, opened his dark eyes wide and rolled them theatrically. Then both boys giggled as if she had asked a stupid question.

'Well,' she said, forcing a smile, 'where does he live?'

'Olentzero, he live in forest,' Joseba said in his halting English. 'He is . . . magique?'

'Magic,' Simon supplied and Joseba nodded so hard that it looked as if his head might come off. All three children grinned at one another with wide eyes and repeated the word. 'Magic!'

'Oh, I see,' Lorna said.

'He come to village to give presents to the children,' Mixel said. 'He is . . . how you say? Papa Noël.'

'Father Christmas?' Simon translated and gave a laugh, then did his best to look and sound superior to these simple French country children. 'But there isn't any Father Christmas. That's just a fairy story for babies. I stopped believing in him a long time ago.'

Well, that was true, anyway. Lorna had so enjoyed pretending to her son that there was such a person. Her neighbour's husband had dressed up in the traditional red cloak and white beard every year and crept into their house at midnight, just so Simon wouldn't lose out. Unfortunately, a couple of years ago, he had caught his beard on the bedpost and revealed his identity to the indignant nine-year-old.

'He is real!' Mixel argued fervently. 'We . . . Joseba and me . . . we have seen him. Maman! Maman!'

There was a soft footfall on the creaking stairs that could only just be heard above the storm that was now raging outside. Carla came back into the room at the same time that Roberto dodged back into the house, shaking off the rain from his head and shoulders.

'What is it, Mixel?' Carla asked.

'We speak of Olentzero. Tell Simon we do not lie.'

Carla seemed momentarily confused. She glared at her son, and then looked beseechingly at her husband. 'Roberto, tell them there is no such person. Olentzero is part of our tradition . . . a legend. He belongs to us, to the Basques. He is not for the . . . the foreign visitors. There is no real person called Olentzero. Please tell them, Roberto.'

Lorna couldn't see why Carla should be so upset at the mention of a mythical character.

★ ★ ★

For the first time, Roberto looked somewhat disconcerted, but then his wife's behaviour was more than a little out of the ordinary. He sat down, suddenly looking much older. The smile, which hardly ever left his face, was forced and did not reach his eyes.

'Olentzero,' he said, and hesitated, while Lorna and the three boys hung on to that one word, wondering what he was going to say about this man who was purported to be magic. 'Well, it is as Carla says. He is a Basque legend. The equivalent to your Father Christmas. History has it that he was a foundling in the forest many centuries ago. He was adopted by the charcoal maker, who was very kind and made him lots of toys out of the wood from the trees. When he was older, Olentzero continued the work of his adoptive father and began making toys for the poor children of the villages all around. Every year at Christmas Eve he brings to the villages the toys he has made.'

'What a lovely story,' Lorna said, and Roberto's smile widened, though it still did not reach his eyes.

'Yes, but it is a story of fiction. The stuff of dreams, eh?'

'He will come the night before

Christmas,' Mixel said and ignored a sharp rebuke from his mother. 'He will. It is true. But if you have something special to ask of him, you must find him in the forest before then.'

'Do not listen to the boy,' Carla said. 'He is foolish to believe all that nonsense.'

'If I find Olentzero,' Simon said, 'I'll ask him if he knows where my father is.'

'Enough!' Carla said to Mixel and Joseba. 'You have your schoolwork to do. Go, please, and do it. Now, I say! Then I need you to help me clean out the goat shed.' She glanced meaningfully at her husband, then at Lorna. 'Excuse me, please. I have much work to do.'

★ ★ ★

'I must apologise for my dear wife,' Roberto said. 'She does not like the dreams of children. It reminds her too much of her own childhood.' He looked across at Simon. 'Well now, my young

118

friend, what are we going to do with you, eh?'

Simon gave a sniff and shrugged his shoulders. Carla had disappointed him just as he was beginning to get his hopes up.

'You mustn't worry about us, Roberto,' Lorna said. 'I know how busy you are. We'll just go back to our room at your mother's and wait for David to arrive.'

'I think you are going to have a long wait,' Roberto told her. 'I look at the sky and I see trouble approaching.'

He didn't say what kind of trouble, but even he wasn't to know what was about to happen next.

Anxiety for Lorna

Madame Lafon's *specialité de la maison* turned out to be a very rich lamb stew with spicy chorizo sausage and sweet peppers, laced with a rich and creamy garlic sauce. The whole family, including Lorna and Simon, and Mixel's friend, Joseba, gathered around the communal table and eyed the dish hungrily. The old lady said a prayer, then broke pieces from a large round loaf of rough dark bread and passed them around, not forgetting a crusty end piece for the vacant place at the head of the table.

'That is for my *papa*,' Roberto whispered to Lorna. 'Always, since the day he left us, *maman* has laid the table as if he was still here.'

'Oh, how sweet,' Lorna said, remembering how she had done much the same for Max the first Christmas he had spent away from home. It had brought her some small measure of comfort.

'Sometimes,' Roberto continued, breaking bread into his stew, 'I swear he is sitting there in his usual place, watching over us all and growling like an old boar when one of us does something he doesn't approve of.'

'Did you not ask Olentzero to find him for you?' Simon asked, and Lorna caught her breath in horror, but nobody seemed to have heard except her and Roberto.

'You cannot find that which is gone forever, Simon,' Roberto said. 'I saw my father die. He was old and sick. It was his time to go. It makes my mother happy to keep the memory of him alive. You must do this too, with your father.'

'But he's not old or sick,' Simon said. 'And he's not dead.'

There was so much confidence in Simon's simple statement that Lorna experienced a prickling all over her skin, just as if Max had passed close by her.

'Eat your food before it gets cold, Simon,' she said sharply.

'*Bon appetit!*' Madame Lafon announced in a loud voice and there was a chorus of responses, followed by a great clattering of spoons on bowls.

'This is so good!' Lorna said, and meant it. She caught the eye of her hostess and beamed a congratulatory smile, which earned her another ladling of the stew.

She received a short nod from the old lady, who did her best to hide her pride in her cuisine behind a brusque manner, which was softening by the hour. She glowed much more openly when she produced a dessert of *Tarte au Basque* with its pastry base, creamy almond filling and crisp golden sponge topping.

It was good to see Simon tucking into his food and socialising. And Lorna was bowled over when he was cheeky enough to suggest that she ask *madame* for the recipes for both dishes. Lorna suspected that he had, perhaps, drunk a little too much of the homemade apple cider that was going around the table in a large brown pottery jug that never seemed to be empty. Lorna knew, by the lightness of her own head, that it was surprisingly potent and saw that the two Basque children had a little water added to theirs by a watchful Roberto.

After the meal, Mixel scrabbled about in one of his grandmother's cupboards and unearthed some small wooden carvings, toys he said Olentzero had given him. Lorna thought she caught a slight uneasy movement from Roberto as the toys were produced, but he said nothing. Simon pounced on one toy in particular, and when he spoke he seemed to be choked with emotion.

'He made this? Olentzero?'

'Yes. It is beautiful, *non*?'

'What is it, darling?' Lorna asked, and Simon passed the object over her.

The toy was a tiny violin, beautifully made to scale, and there were strings and a matching bow, all carved out of the palest, honey-coloured pinewood.

'Olentzero made this, Mum,' he said, inspecting it with such an expression in his eyes that she thought, for one awful moment, he was going to burst into tears.

Then the most unexpected thing happened. Simon gave back the miniature toy violin and rushed upstairs, returning minutes later with the violin he had insisted on bringing with him. He tucked it under his chin and, to the astonishment of all who were present, played the first few haunting notes of a Bruch serenade.

Lorna drew in a gasp of astonishment as she recognised, not her son's instrument, but Max's. Simon had dared to bring the priceless Stradivarius. She would have words with him about that later. But not now.

Simon's performance was far from perfect, but she was so proud of him that she joined in the hearty applause as he struggled to the end of the *andante con moto*. He lowered the instrument with a self-conscious blush. Lorna had never heard him play so well.

★　★　★

Full of good food and gratitude, Lorna was ready for bed long before nine struck on the big corner clock in the hall. Roberto and Carla and the two Basque children took their leave. Everyone seemed particularly tired. Simon did not need any persuasion to accompany Lorna to their room. He seemed unusually quiet as she tucked him in his cot bed, but put it down to the rich food, the cider and the exhilaration. She hoped he would not be sick at some unearthly hour in the middle of the night.

'Mum?' She was just drifting off to sleep herself, when she heard his whisper through the darkness. 'You don't really believe that my father is dead, do you?'

'Oh, Simon . . . ' She flopped on to

her side and stared blindly in his direction, though she could see nothing but a black void. 'I wish you would stop beating yourself up about this. Don't you think that if your father was still alive, I would know about it?'

But Simon wasn't listening to her. He spoke in a voice that was half asleep and dreamy.

'I'm going to find Olentzero and ask him to find my dad,' he said. 'Mixel and Joseba say there isn't anything Olentzero can't do.'

★   ★   ★

The following morning, Mixel and Joseba sat stiffly upright at the table in Madame Lafon's kitchen. Roberto was on his feet, leaning on his fists, one of which kept pounding the scrubbed wooden surface as he plied the boys with questions that they couldn't, or wouldn't, answer.

'*Mon Dieu*, but you must know *something*! Simon would not wander off on his own in the middle of the night. Not in a storm!' The fist banged, the cutlery and dishes rattled, and the boys flinched, but they were not about to divulge anything. 'Come! Do not play the innocent with me. Where has he gone?'

Lorna watched the scene in silence. The shock of finding Simon missing from his bed that morning and nowhere to be found in the house had left her feeling numb.

Out of the corner of her eye she saw Carla in much the same shocked state. The dark, Hispanic eyes flashed wildly from Mixel to Joseba, but only briefly rested on Lorna herself. Roberto's wife was acting as guiltily as the two boys.

'We don't know, *Papa*,' Mixel shook his head vehemently and his friend copied the action with even more emphasis. 'That's true, *Monsieur Lafon*. He said nothing to us.'

Lorna looked at the half-case clock on the wall. It was eight-twenty, and outside, the storm was raging with renewed vigour, making the day look dark and ominous.

Carla made an impatient gesture with her hands and left the room. No-one took any notice of her. All attention was focussed on the two boys. Mixel and Joseba looked more cautious than scared. They constantly exchanged furtive glances while their father interrogated them.

On finding Simon missing, Lorna had, in the first instance, demanded that the police be sent for. However, this was apparently out of the question. The only phone, installed in the schoolhouse, was dead, the lines having been brought down by the storm. And, as Roberto had been at pains to explain to her, as the schoolmaster and mayor, it was his responsibility to sort out the business of the missing boy.

Roberto now threw his hands in the air and turned to Lorna.

'I am sure they know something,' he said, 'but what do I do? Beat them until they tell me what I want to know? They have done wrong, but they are good boys.'

Lorna tried to force herself to relax, trying to convince herself that Simon's disappearance was nothing sinister. She wasn't persuaded that the boys had actually had a hand in it. It had surely been Simon's idea to go. But go where? Into the forest, where it was frighteningly dark and there was a storm crashing about all around him? Simon didn't like the dark any more than she did. And yet, what other explanation could there be?

'I don't know where he's gone,' she said, 'but I think I know why he's run off.'

'It has to be Mixel and Joseba's fault,' Roberto said grimly.

'No!' The two boys cried out simultaneously.

'I think they're telling the truth, Roberto,' Lorna said, sinking into the nearest chair and accepting a small glass of Armagnac from Madame Lafon, who saw fit to pat her shoulder in a maternal gesture.

'But where can he have gone?' Roberto said.

'I think he's gone to find this character called Olentzero,' Lorna said. 'The last thing he said to me when we went to bed last night was that he was going to seek out this character and ask him to find his father for him.'

'This is all your doing!' Roberto pointed an accusing finger at Mixel and Joseba, who shrank back from him.

'I don't think so, Roberto.' Lorna could not let him go on blaming the two boys. 'If they had a hand in it, they would have gone with Simon, surely.'

What she said seemed to make sense to Roberto. He gave one final glare at the boys and then indicated, with a slight flick of his head, that they should leave the room. They took no second telling, and fled.

Roberto's mother placed a platter of freshly baked *brioche* on the table, together with a pot of honey and a jug of coffee.

'*Mangez, madame!*' she said, ordering Lorna to eat, and fixing her son with the same commanding eye.

Roberto sank down on a chair opposite Lorna and helped himself to one of the large, cake-like buns.

The appetising aroma of warm vanilla filled the room, but Lorna had no appetite. She might have enjoyed sampling her first brioche had it not been for her anxious state. Simon was being difficult, but he was, on the whole, a sensible child. Once he realised how impossible his mission was, he would return, wet, miserable and shamefaced.

'Do you know where to look?' she asked Roberto, and he nodded.

'It is a long time since . . . ' He shook his head, and then changed his mind when he saw her worried expression. 'There is a young man in the village. He can take us to Olentzero, if that becomes necessary.'

'Do you mean to say that this character actually does exist?'

'Oh, but yes! There are many Olentzeros in the Basque country.'

'I don't understand. I thought they were nothing more than fiction . . . an ancient legend.'

Roberto laughed softly. 'Yes, that is also true. Like your Santa Claus, and the French Papa Noël. Here in the Pyrenees we have Olentzero, the charcoal maker, who lives alone in the forest. All year round he makes the charcoal for our fires and toys for our children. Oh, my English friend, he is very real. Very real indeed, even if he is not the original character of the myth. And many believe that such a man did exist, although the stories we hear vary from valley to valley.'

'And do you, Roberto, believe in all this . . . this magic?'

'Ah! No, in magic I do not believe. But I do believe in good, and anyone who takes on the name and the role of Olentzero is a good man and does good for the people.'

'It is not just the children he helps.

There are many good deeds that the simple peasant might see as miracles. Some think that Olentzero has the ability to become invisible, for they do not see him carrying out his work — a mended fence here, a new cart there. He even seems to be able to heal sick animals.'

Lorna shook her head. 'He must be an incredible human being.'

'That is true, but ... ' Roberto frowned down at his empty plate and rubbed a hand over his unshaven chin.

'But?'

'Nothing! I am sure we will not have far to go to find your son.'

★ ★ ★

The young man who was to guide them was called André Ducau. He was the local carpenter.

'André was a foundling, just like the original Olentzero,' Roberto said, slapping the young man on the back. 'There isn't much about the forest he does not know. If anyone can find your son, it is him.'

'And if he can't find him?'

'Then we will go to Olentzero, for he is the only one who can find his way through the deepest areas of the forest.'

'In that case, let's not waste any more time,' Lorna said, starting to get up from her chair,. She was stopped by Roberto holding up the palm of his hand and shaking his head.

'First, you must eat, as my mother commanded. With food in your belly you will have the energy to look for Simon. Without it, you are no use to him, to me, or to yourself.'

Lorna did as she was told and managed to eat the best part of a brioche, but, delicious though it was, she had difficulty swallowing the soft cake bread.

'I was hoping that David would be back today,' she said, then followed Roberto's gaze to the window, knowing that her hope had been in vain.

'The storm will keep him at St Jean

Pied de Port. He would be foolish to attempt the journey. I will ask Carla to look out for him and tell him what has happened.'

As if he had conjured her up, his wife suddenly appeared in the room. When she spoke, it was obvious that there was a problem. The couple appeared to be arguing again, but it was all so rapid there wasn't one recognisable word in their discourse. Carla also seemed a little more than put out. Lorna thought she saw panic in those dark gypsy eyes.

'What is it, Roberto?' she asked, after Carla had stormed out, slamming the door behind her. 'Carla seems upset about something.'

'Don't worry,' Roberto said. 'It is just her way. She is very highly strung.'

'That may be so, Roberto,' Lorna stared at the door, still seeing Roberto's wife in her mind's eye, still feeling the intensity of the girl's odd behaviour, 'but ever since we arrived, Carla has acted as though we were somehow the enemy.'

'*Mon Dieu, non!*' Roberto threw his hands in the air. 'How can this be? No, I will tell you what it is. She is still very much a child in her head. She still believes in the magic of Olentzero and the tradition that no-one must see him during the days that lead up to Noël. It is said to bring bad luck on the family.'

'She is very superstitious?'

'We French are a superstitious race.'

'Roberto, are you telling me the truth?' She had to ask, because into the teacher's kindly eyes had come a strange and worrying light.

'We will say no more now,' he said, ignoring her question. 'But I have decided that it is too dangerous for you to come with us. Better you stay here, in case the boy returns.'

'Oh, but . . . ' Lorna started to object; she needed to do something positive, not sit helplessly waiting at home for news, like she did for Max.

'You will only hamper us. Please, do as I ask and stay here. My mother will look after you. Do not upset yourself,

Lorna. I will find the boy.'

'I take it you're not superstitious then?' Lorna could not keep a certain sharpness out of her voice. 'Aren't you afraid you might come across this Olentzero and bring bad luck on your family?'

Roberto simply smiled and left without uttering a further word.

Madame Lafon came back into the room and fussed over Lorna, making sympathetic murmurings that needed no translation. She understood how the Englishwoman was feeling.

After a while, Lorna decided to go and wait in the room upstairs that she shared with Simon. She could worry there in private, and being close to his belongings was somehow comforting. The trouble was, she no sooner entered the room than she noticed something that had escaped her earlier.

Something was missing. The Stradivarius.

That was when the numbing shock of Simon's disappearance wore off and emotion kicked in. She sat down heavily on the bed, making the springs jangle and complain. The tears she had kept at bay now coursed down her cheeks.

She had lost the husband she worshipped. She couldn't also lose the child he had given her. *She couldn't!*

Downstairs there were voices, Madame Lafon's and a young male voice she didn't recognise. They were speaking in the strange Basque tongue that sounded like no other language she had ever heard before, and they were very animated.

'*Madame, Madame!*' Feet thundered on the stairs and someone rapped hard on her door. 'Please to open. It is André Ducau.'

She pulled open the door immediately on recognising the name. It was the young man from the village who was supposed to be helping Roberto search for her son.

'What is it? Have you found him already?'

The youth shook his dark curly head,

sprinkling her with raindrops. His face was tanned and rosy from a healthy outdoor life.

'Found him? No! Carla . . . Madame Roberto Lafon . . . she tell me not to go. She say message is from Monsieur Lafon.'

'Then why are you here? I don't understand.'

'Carla no tell truth. She lie . . . all the time she lie.'

'Why would she lie, André? What is this big secret she has that makes her so unfriendly towards us?'

André shrugged his broad shoulders. 'She is . . . how you say . . . *folle?*'

'Foolish? Crazy?'

'Crazy, yes! When she was young, she got lost in the forest. Olentzero find her. She stay with him some days, then he bring her home. But she make him a promise that she will never tell people how to find him.'

'But Roberto knows where this Olentzero can be found.'

André shook his head. 'Perhaps,

perhaps not. It is long years since he visited with Olentzero. But I, André Ducau, I know where is the charcoal maker.'

'You do?'

'Yes. I follow Carla one day when she take food to Olentzero. Later, I go see Olentzero and ask him to show me how to work with the wood.' André stopped. 'He is like father to me. Some day, when the time comes, I will be Olentzero.'

Lorna stared at him for a brief instant, then rushed to fetch her warmest clothes. 'André, you must take me to him. Take me to Olentzero.'

'He will not like you to see him,' André replied, and then nodded. 'But, yes, I will take you.'

'You're not afraid?' She repeated the same question she had put to Roberto. 'I mean . . . this superstition about seeing him bringing bad luck on your family?'

André grinned.

'No. I am not afraid of Olentzero. He

140

is good man. Last year he help me when my house collapse in storm. Olentzero is good friend to people in trouble.'

'Well,' said Lorna, winding a long scarf around her neck, 'he's certainly going to have his hands full today.'

'We go?'

'Yes, André,' Lorna said. 'We go.'

A Mystery Solved

Lorna followed closely in André's sure footsteps. He knew she was no mountain goat and went at a reasonable pace to accommodate her. Even so, it was difficult walking through the storm-wracked forest. Thunder and lightning crashed above the treetops that were being whipped by the wind with such force that they bent like twigs and looked in danger of snapping.

The ground underfoot was soft and slippery, so that their feet were sucked down, and there were rogue branches and exposed roots to grab at their ankles and hold them back like dark, spirit hands.

Lorna bent her head and forged onwards and upwards in the direction of the densely wooded foothills. She did not think, dared not allow herself to think, what she was doing and why. The worst scenario would be that they would not find Simon.

Seeing the gap between herself and the young Basque widen, Lorna stopped, gasping for breath and choking as she swallowed wind and water. She rested a moment, propping herself against the rough bark of a giant umbrella pine. Her heart was pounding in her chest, the blood pulsating in her ears. When she lifted her hand to wipe the rainwater from her face, she noticed that her fingers were shaking.

'*Madame?*' André, realising that she was no longer keeping up with him, had backtracked and was standing over her, eyes full of concern. 'We rest . . . two minutes, *non?*'

'No!' she shook her head and pushed herself away from the tree. 'Let's keep going.'

★   ★   ★

They had been walking a little over an hour and there was nothing to see but dense forest all around them. Behind them, the tiny hamlet of Mendibel lay nestling in the valley, long gone from sight beneath a misty shroud.

It was all so surreal. Lorna half believed that she was locked in a dream and would wake up back home in her chintzy English lounge with Simon practising his violin in the next room. And later, David coming to tea, expecting a positive response to his new proposal of marriage.

And the next time it happened, if it happened at all, she would say 'yes', because she was tired of this limbo space she seemed to be occupying. She was sure that, in time, Simon would come to accept the situation.

★ ★ ★

The cry was very faint. At first, Lorna thought she was imagining things. Then, to her left, she thought she saw a light moving from side to side, appearing and disappearing through the lower branches of the fir trees.

She wasn't mistaken. There was the cry again and what looked like a torch beam. The cry was faint and the light, although moving, did not get any closer. Whoever it was, they were holding their position while trying to attract attention. She was sure, however, that it was not Simon.

'André!' Lorna yelled the youth's name at the top of her voice. 'There's someone over there . . . look!'

She had to call out several times before André heard her because the wind kept carrying her voice away. He eventually looked over his shoulder and slithered to a halt, for the land had begun to plunge downhill through frantically bubbling streams and flowing waterfalls.

She pointed just as there was another cry. This time it was unmistakable. It was a man and it was obvious that he was in difficulties.

They walked sideways like sand crabs, clinging on to the sodden undergrowth for support, André going first as always, keeping an eye on Lorna and offering her his hand if he felt she needed help.

He swore loudly as they came across the prone figure pinned down by a fallen conifer which lay across his back, pressing him face down into the swirling mud of a narrow track. 'Roberto!'

'André?' Roberto's voice was rough, coarsened by pain. 'What happened? Carla told me you could not come.'

'Carla has problem in the head, my friend,' André told him, as he assessed the situation, his frown deepening all the while.

'I must speak with her,' Roberto whispered, his voice fading. 'I must . . . get help for her.'

He appeared to be at the end of his tether, for as they approached, he sank into a semi-conscious state and the torch fell from his grasp, rolling through the mud and coming to rest at Lorna's feet.

'Is he badly hurt, do you think?'

Lorna shouted through the storm as André bent over their friend.

'I cannot tell. We must lift the tree from him.'

As he spoke, he moved to one end of the tree and encircled it with his arms. Lorna saw him strain, muscles bulging. The tree moved hardly a centimetre. She went to stand beside him, mirroring his actions, but even between them they could not shift the tree from Roberto's still body.

'André, what do we do now?' Lorna asked. 'We've got to get help.'

'I will go. You stay here with Roberto.'

'But where are you going? Back to Mendibel?'

'No. Is too far. I go on.' He indicated the next rise ahead of them.

'But where to, André? There's nothing out there.'

'There is Olentzero. He will help.'

'How can he help?'

'You do not know Olentzero.'

'But I thought he didn't like to be seen.'

'That is true. But is nothing to do with magic or superstition. A bad thing happened to him during the war. He . . . ' André pulled himself up and stepped away from her. 'Is long story. I go.'

He set off at a pace much faster than he had travelled so far. It was almost a gazelle-type run, his long muscular legs carrying him so fast that he hardly seemed to touch the ground.

Lorna watched him until she could no longer see his figure flitting through the green curtain of pine trees. Then she turned back to Roberto, who had uttered a slight moaning sound.

'Try to hang on, Roberto,' she said, gently wiping his mud-spattered face with her damp handkerchief. 'André's gone for help.'

There was very little Lorna could do. Her attempt at conversation was drowned out by the storm, that was going from bad to worse. She sat in the freezing mud and took hold of one of Roberto's hands, holding it firmly in both of hers.

She felt that it perhaps gave them both a little comfort.

She lost track of time. The sky continued to boil in shades of grey and purple and, despite it being some time around midday, it seemed more like night there in that dark green nightmare of a place.

★　★　★

At long last she knew they were no longer alone when she saw a big white Pyrenean mountain dog bound towards them, barking madly. It was a younger version of the one at Madame Lafon's house, and impressively more powerful. She stiffened with instant fear, but it suddenly stopped its barking and began sniffing and whining, running in circles all around the spot where they were.

If anyone spoke to the animal she did not hear it, but two figures emerged not far behind the dog. One was unmistakably André. The other, taller, broader and dressed strangely like some old mountain man in animal skins and hessian, walked with his hand on the youth's shoulder.

'See, *madame*!' André's eyes sparkled with unbridled pride. 'I have brought Olentzero to you. He will help free Roberto.'

The man he called Olentzero did not look up, but even with his hooded head kept low and in shadow, he was a good few inches taller than André.

It was only when he started passing his hands over Roberto and the tree that lay across him, that Lorna realised that Olentzero was blind.

★　★　★

'Oh, I'm so glad André found you, monsieur,' she said, scrambling up stiffly. At the sound of her voice, the big charcoal maker looked up, then shook his head and silently continued with his inspection of the situation.

Ignoring Lorna, Olentzero made various pointing motions with his long, tapering fingers that would not have looked out of place on an artist. André seemed to understand and took up position near where Roberto lay, telling Lorna to be ready to help pull him free.

She hardly believed they would manage without the help of a crane of some sort, but the thought was hardly formed in her head when Olentzero took hold of the tree and heaved, just as André had done earlier. He did not make it look easy, but the tree came up slowly and surely, allowing them space and time to drag Roberto clear.

The man of the forest released the tree with a satisfied grunt. He paused to caress his dog, which pressed itself to his thigh, and then he was feeling for Roberto again. With minimal effort he lifted him in his arms as he would a small child.

'Come!' he said gruffly in English, setting out ahead of them, the dog trotting close to his side, occasionally nudging the man to keep him on course.

'I can't believe it,' Lorna said to André, who had taken her arm and was helping her down a treacherous hill that the big, older man took in his long stride. 'Did he really lift that tree all on his own?'

André laughed and nodded. 'We Basques are famous for our strength,' he said, 'but Olentzero, he is exceptional.'

'Did you tell him that we are looking for my son?'

She thought she detected a small hesitation before he responded, 'He knows of your son, yes.'

He said no more and she did not ply him with more questions as they walked, slipped, slithered and climbed through the forest, following narrow tracks that were barely visible. She had no more strength for conversation. André, too, had fallen silent, and the famous *Monsieur Olentzero* did not show any indication that he wanted to talk.

★　★　★

The fatigue already brought on by the strenuous journey was now added to, along with the frustration of not being able to carry on with the search for Simon. Trudging wearily along behind the silent bear of a man, Lorna was tempted to rant and rave at him, and demand that he look for Simon.

How sad, was that, she thought! Here was a simple forester possibly saving the life of Roberto Lafon and she was being selfish. But her son was only eleven years old, lost in a storm in the vast forest of Iraty. And it was a forest that seemed to grow more and more vast with every step they took.

'We have arrived!' André, some yards ahead of her now, turned and beckoned, pointing to a broader track between the trees where the light seemed brighter and the leaves and grass a more vibrant green.

He loped back to her side and gave her a helping hand for the rest of the way.

★　　★　　★

There was a squat, wattle and daub cottage, its ancient timbers plastered between rough timber support beams with clay the colour of cinder toffee. A welcoming light shone from its one tiny window, at which yellow curtains hung, giving it a sunny aspect. Lorna had expected a hovel, not curtains. After all, Olentzero couldn't see them or appreciate the way they must make his dark dwelling glow with the colour of the sun.

All the time they had walked, the big Basque had kept his face averted, the hood of his cloak hiding the features she was curious to see. However, it was perhaps just as well. Roberto had mentioned that something terrible had happened to the man during the war. Perhaps he had some kind of disfigurement he wanted to keep hidden, a scar perhaps, or a burn. Whatever the reason, she should not pre-judge the man, especially if he was going to help her find her son.

As they approached the cottage, Lorna was even more amazed to see the battered wooden door swing open with a flourish. A small figure bounded out, then halted uncertainly. It was none other than Simon, looking dirty and with a tear in his jacket, and another in the knee of his trousers. He stared at his mother and bit his bottom lip with all the guilt of a truant schoolboy.

'Simon! Oh, my goodness, you're safe!' Lorna was too relieved to be angry. That could come later. Now, all she wanted to do was take him in her arms and hug him tightly.

'Oh, Mum, don't!' He squirmed away from her grasp, and then grinned sheepishly. 'I'm sorry I ran away, but I did find Olentzero. Isn't he amazing!'

'Please . . . come in.' Olentzero was already inside the cottage and had placed Roberto on a bench.

'Come on, Mum.' Simon tugged at her hand, trying to pull her into the warm interior that was slightly smoky because of the big open wood fire.

Lorna hesitated. There was something about Olentzero's deep, rich voice that made the hairs on her arms prickle. She gave a shiver and followed Simon inside.

She was further amazed to find the place clean and surprisingly tidy. It was a living space and a workshop all in one. There were wide shelves lining the walls, filled with toys carved from wood.

So, the man was what they said he was, after all, and not just a simple peasant making charcoal in the forest. He obviously had the expertise to turn a piece of wood into something beautiful. There was evidence of that everywhere.

'Look!' Simon pointed to one shelf full of small violins in various stages of completion. The other shelves held an assortment of carved animals; bears, sheep and goats. And one or two Pyrenean Mountain Dogs like the one leaping joyously at Simon right now.

'Please . . . sit down,' Olentzero commanded, indicating the chairs around the table as he bent over Roberto and prodded him gently, causing the teacher to groan and wince.

'Is he going to be all right?' Lorna felt she had to ask, needed to talk to this man, was desperate to hear more of his voice, which was causing her such alarm.

'No broken bones, I think,' the big man said, pulling a thick woollen blanket over Roberto, who was looking pale and in discomfort, but was at least conscious and trying to smile.

'Oh, Roberto,' Lorna knelt down beside him with a sigh. 'I feel responsible for this. If Simon had not taken it into his head to run off like that, this would never have happened.'

'Do not worry, Lorna,' Roberto tried to move and gave a gasp of pain. 'I am indestructible. Anyway, the boy has been found, thanks to Olentzero here.'

'I've asked him . . . you know . . . ' Simon came to stand beside his mother, hands stuffed into his trouser pockets, 'about my father.'

Lorna saw how Olentzero was listening to the conversation, even though his back was turned as he stirred a cauldron of soup on a grid over the log fire. His big shoulders seemed to hunch even more and he stopped stirring, as if waiting for her reply.

'And what did he say?' Lorna asked, keeping her eyes fixed on the Basque charcoal maker.

'He said I should forget my father and go back to England, because . . . ' Simon's eyes grew unnaturally bright and she saw his chin quiver. 'He says my father died a long time ago.'

'Perhaps Olentzero is right, Simon. We should go home.'

What else could she say? This man, this strange, mysterious individual, could no more make miracles happen than their own Santa Claus. He did good work; she had no doubt about that. The people had adopted him, made him their living Olentzero, but he was, after all, just a man.

The man in question slowly filled a bowl with chicken broth and came with it to where Roberto was lying. He bent over his patient. Lorna reached out and took the bowl and spoon from him.

'Let me,' she said, noticing again the long, beautiful hands that were still beautiful despite the scars and calluses caused by his carpentry.

He straightened up a little too suddenly, almost as if being so close to her caused him pain. The jerky movement disturbed the hood he still wore.

There were no horrible disfigurements, as she had expected, apart from a faint scar across one cheekbone. His eyes were the deepest shade of blue that not even his blindness had diminished. They seemed to be staring straight at her, yet she could tell that they saw nothing.

Lorna's throat contracted and her heart tumbled about in her chest, unable to continue beating normally. She tried to speak, but all she could do was swallow dryly as full realisation hit her.

Her eyes darted to her son, then back to the man standing before her. A man she had believed to be dead.

How could she explain to Simon that Olentzero was, in fact, his long-lost father? The son had searched for the father, but in the end it was the father who had found the son.

'Max!' she whispered, as the soup bowl tumbled from her numb fingers and broke into pieces on the wooden floor, spilling its contents at her feet.

Denial

'You are mistaken, *madame*.' The words Olentzero spoke were firm and unwavering. He had replaced his hood and was once again moving about the cottage with his back turned. Lorna was still too shocked to go to him, too shocked even to see her son's questioning gaze.

'A wife doesn't mistake the face she loved so much, even if it is years since we were together.' She got to her feet, ignoring the shattered dish and the mess of broth on the floor. 'How can you deny who you are? How can you rob your son of the father he has never met? He has always worshipped you, even without knowing you.'

'Son? I have no son! I have no wife.'

He beat his fist down on the table and shook his head vigorously. His hair was long, showing signs of greying, as was his beard. But there was no doubt in Lorna's mind that this was Maxwell Barrett, the famous musician she had married fifteen years ago, and not some crazy, fictitious character from a children's fairytale.

'Lorna . . . ' Roberto's voice was feeble. 'Please stop. There are things you do not know about . . . about Olentzero.'

He tried to sit up, but fell back with a gasp of pain and, once more, Olentzero was there at his side.

'You must see a doctor,' he said gruffly. 'There may be internal injuries. André!'

'*Oui Olentzero?*' André was waiting for his orders, though it was obvious that the exchange between the English woman and his sainted hero had left him dumbfounded.

'Prepare the cart. We will take Roberto home.'

'But the storm, Olentzero.' André looked perturbed. 'The donkey will never make it. She will be frightened.'

'Cover her eyes. She knows the way blindfold, just as I do.' His hand now rested on the smooth head of his dog. 'Zingaro, here, will lead us. You must go ahead to tell the people of your village.'

'And Madame Barrett and the boy? What of them?'

'The woman and the child must stay here.' As he spoke, Lorna started to protest, but he whipped around and stared sightlessly at her. 'No argument, madame. I will come for you later. My first priority is to get this injured man to a doctor.'

'He is right, Madame Barrett,' André said as he hurried out, carrying blankets and a waterproof tarpaulin. 'You will be safe and warm here until Olentzero returns.'

'Keep the door bolted,' Olentzero said, as he once more lifted Roberto and followed the young Basque out into the storm. 'Tonight is a night when wild animals search for somewhere dry and warm. We do not want them feeding on you.'

Lorna hoped that his last remark was a touch of humour, but he looked deadly serious.

*   *   *

She could find no words to say. Her mind, her whole system, had shut down. As the door closed, she went to it and pulled the big iron bolt into place, and then backed away, listening to the voices outside that became gradually muted as they moved further away.

'Mum?' It was a faint, tremulous whisper.

As Lorna stood, traumatised by the last few minutes, her gaze fixed hypnotically on the worn timbers of the door, she could hardly believe that she had forgotten Simon's presence. He touched her and she turned, wanting to hold him close, but not daring to, fearing rejection.

'Simon, I don't know what to say.'

She heard his sharp intake of breath; saw the confusion in his eyes as he waited for an explanation of what had just taken place.

'You called him Max . . . ' he said. 'That's my father's name.'

'Yes, Simon.' She hesitated for a long moment and her son waited while she attempted to gather her thoughts. 'The man you call Olentzero . . . '

'Yes?'

'That man who just left here is Maxwell Barrett, your father.'

'But he can't be! Everybody knows him. Mixel and Joseba have known him for years, like all the other children around here. They described him to me. That's how I knew who he was when I found him.'

'When you found him?'

'Well, not exactly . . . ' Simon hung his head and picked at the tear in his jacket. 'I tripped and rolled down a steep bank. Zingaro found me and led me here to Olentzero's cottage. I knew right away who he was. He was sitting carving a piece of wood when I arrived and there were piles of charcoal stacked up everywhere.'

'Perhaps people do know that man as Olentzero, Simon. But I tell you, sweetheart, that is the man I married. He is your father.'

'Then why is he pretending he doesn't know you?'

It was a question she couldn't answer. Perhaps, when he got back, he would explain everything. She certainly had plenty to ask him.

'I don't understand . . . ' Simon started to speak again, but Lorna cut him off abruptly.

'Neither do I, Simon, so don't ask me any more questions, all right?' The sharpness of her rebuke made the child flinch and he looked close to tears. 'Oh, sweetheart, I'm sorry! I don't know what's happening any more than you do, believe me. Let's just wait and see what he says when he gets back, eh?'

In the meantime, what were they going to do? Lorna asked herself. However long it took for him to get back, would seem like an eternity. To see Max like that, without warning, when all these years she had thought him to be dead, it was more than her brain could cope with, not to say what it was doing to her heart. And he had looked at her with those same lovely eyes of his, that were now sightless, and denied that he knew her.

But she must keep calm, for the sake of her son. It was just such a pity that he had stumbled across Max the way he had. Maybe it would have been better had he never met him. They could have gone back to England and got on with their lives. And yet . . . oh, how could she think like that!

Lorna stemmed a sob of frustration. Going back to England and getting on with their lives was no longer an option. Though where they would go from here, she had no idea.

'Look,' Simon had recovered from her rebuff and was making a tour of the cottage. 'He makes violins. Not just toy ones, Mum. He makes real ones . . . see?'

He held up a half-made violin to show her and a lump arose in her throat.

'He was always very good at making violins,' she told him. 'His father taught him.'

'My grandfather?'

'Yes. You never knew him, but he was a lovely old man. He played the violin, too. It was always his ambition that his son should play better than he did. He lived just long enough to see your father perform in his first concert.'

'Do you think my father will be pleased to hear that I play the violin?'

Lorna smiled and stroked her son's cheek. 'I'm sure he will, Simon. How could he not be proud of you?'

'And you're sure that Olentzero is my dad?'

'One hundred per cent sure, love. Nobody else has a voice like Maxwell Barrett, and I remember those eyes so well. Just like yours.'

'Wow!' For a moment, Simon looked as if he might cry, then a smile cracked his face in two. 'Wait till Mixel and Joseba and their friends find out that I am the son of the great Olentzero!'

There was no clock in the cottage and Lorna had not stopped to put on her watch when she had rushed out that morning in search of Simon, so she had no idea how long they waited.

The storm, after endlessly battering the cottage and the trees all around, had eventually abated. The sky lightened, letting through a watery ray of sunshine before dusk finally encroached. The forest fell silent, except for the constant drip of rainwater and some unidentified rustling in the bushes as some wild animal foraged.

'He *is* going to come back, isn't he?' Simon asked fearfully.

'Of course, silly,' Lorna said with an encouraging smile. 'He lives here.'

Minutes later they both jumped to their feet at the sound of plodding hoofs and the creak of cartwheels. As the sound grew closer, they heard Zingaro's bark and the response of his master. Then Olentzero was beating on the door.

★   ★   ★

Lorna pulled back the heavy bolt with difficulty and stepped back, letting the door swing open. She needed to have distance between them. Being so close to Max, after so long, she would be unable not to throw herself into his arms. Simon stood to one side, uncertain how to behave in the circumstances, and she empathised fully with him.

'Roberto?' She managed to get that one word out and her voice cracked. 'How is he?'

The broad back was already turned to her as Olentzero replenished the wood on the fire, which she had kept going in his absence. At least, she thought, he was no longer hiding beneath his hood.

'He is in good hands. The telephone cable has been repaired and an ambulance came to take him to hospital.' He turned to face her and shrugged out of his cape, draping it over the back of a chair. 'It was just a precaution, but the doctor who came with the ambulance thought there was nothing of great concern.'

'How did you get to be so strong, Olentzero?'

Lorna was glad that Simon had not called Max, 'father'. She didn't know why, but she suspected that this was something that had to be handled with great care until she knew the full story behind this strange man of the forest who, she knew, had once been her husband.

She saw the big man sigh and shake his head, but his expression softened at the sound of Simon's voice. He took off yet another layer of clothes, a roughly designed jacket made of goatskin. Beneath his thick, woollen shirt, his body was firm and muscular.

'Do you prefer to be known as Olentzero?' Lorna asked.

'That is the only name I know,' he said.

'But . . . ' No, Lorna, be careful! 'You are English.'

'Yes, it appears that I am English, though I haven't spoken English for many years.'

'So, what is your English name?'

The broad shoulders shrugged and he turned away, picking up a long poker and stoking the fire, taking longer over the task than was necessary. After staring sightlessly into the leaping flames, he straightened his back and leaned against the rustic oak mantelshelf.

'When they found me in the high forests of Iraty, I was in a terrible state. I had nothing, no clothes, no identification. Worst of all, I had no memory.'

'None at all?'

'Nothing but vague shadows that flitted so quickly through my mind I couldn't grasp them.' His shoulders rose and fell as he looked back on a time he would almost certainly rather forget. 'I remembered the noise of the aircraft engines, the cries of the men with me. I remembered that . . . too well.'

'Roberto Lafon was one of the people who found me. They took me to Olentzero. I apparently lay between life and death for a long time, but always they cared for me, hid me from the Germans.'

'That must have been frightening.'

'The most frightening thing was not remembering who I was. When I was well enough, they told me that I must have been burning when I parachuted out of the plane. All they found were a few scraps of parachute material in the branches of the tree where I had landed.'

'But why didn't they report you . . . an English airman?'

'The enemy, the Gestapo, were everywhere. The people of Mendibel risked their lives to hide me from them. I owe them everything.'

'But why did you not have identification?'

'Who knows?' Again the shoulders rose and fell in a shrug that was more Gallic than English. 'I remember nothing, except being in a plane and then . . . an explosion. We fell from the sky. Everyone was screaming. There were flames . . . ' He rubbed the back of his right hand and she saw the burn scars for the first time. 'Then I woke up here, in this Basque cottage, with an old man bending over me, tending my wounds.'

'Olentzero?'

His face relaxed and he smiled. 'The Olentzero of that time, yes.'

'But *you* are Olentzero,' Simon said from his shadowy corner. The boy had been listening with rapt attention to their conversation. Now, he felt the need to be part of it.

Max shook his head sadly. 'No. The old charcoal maker took me in, looked after me, and taught me his trade. Making charcoal wasn't the only thing he did. You have seen the carvings I have done for the children? I couldn't have done that without his patient teaching.'

'They're beautiful, but . . . ' Lorna gasped for breath. 'What happened to the original Olentzero?'

'He was a good man. He loved children, loved to make them happy at Christmas time. He made me swear that I would continue his work. You see, he taught me how to live without my eyes and . . . Well, how could I not give him this promise that was so important to him? He already knew he was dying. The children could not be disappointed.'

'And yet . . . ' Lorna said, treading warily, 'don't you remember anything from your past? Anything at all?'

'Nothing!'

'Oh, Max . . . ' Lorna sighed as she uttered his name under her breath, but the man sitting a few feet away from her did not appear to hear it. 'I'm so sorry!'

'No! Don't be sorry for me. I have a good life here in the forest. What man could ask for more? England is dead for me. The local Basque people have adopted me as their patron saint of Christmas. I am proud to bear the name of Olentzero. The children do not know that the man they knew previously as Olentzero is dead. They must never find out. You see, Olentzero must go on forever . . . unlike your husband, madame, who lies dead and buried somewhere in the deep forest with his compatriots.'

He was talking in riddles. It was as if he was refusing to accept that he *was* her husband, and yet he must know that she spoke the truth about his identity.

Suddenly, Simon surged forward, taking Lorna and, indeed, Olentzero, by surprise. He beat his small fists on the broad chest of the man who was his father, with a loud cry of disbelief.

'You're lying! You're lying!' He drew back and tears flooded his cheeks. 'I came to look for my father, because I couldn't believe that he was dead. Mum says that *you* are my father, so why are you lying to us?'

Lorna grabbed hold of the back of her son's pullover and hauled him away, wrapping her arms about him tightly, kissing the top of his head until he subsided into a soft mass against her.

The big man got to his feet. 'Get your things. It is time I took you back to the village.'

'No! Wait!' Simon broke away from his mother and rushed to the violin case he had brought with him. '*Please*! You've got to listen to this.'

He pulled out the violin and retreated with it to the far corner of the room.

'Play, Simon,' Lorna encouraged softly. 'Show your father what a gifted son he has.'

★   ★   ★

Simon's hands were shaking as he placed the violin under his chin and struck the first notes of the only concerto he had practised since taking

177

up the instrument at the age of eight. To Lorna, the music was sweet, though to the celebrated musician that her husband had been, it would undoubtedly sound clumsy.

'Stop, stop!' Olentzero clamped his hands over his ears and shook his head as if he were in pain.

The notes that Simon was attempting to play faded and died. He stood, looking at the man before him, an expression of despair shadowing his face.

'I made some mistakes,' he said in a whispery voice. 'Can I start again . . . please, Olentzero? I can do better than this.'

'Who am I to judge? I just want you to stop that caterwauling.'

'Come, I will take you back to Mendibel before it is too late.'

Lorna saw Simon slump with despair and her heart sank with him.

'Max,' she said, watching for some kind of response to his proper name, but there was none. 'This is your son who stands before you. He was playing your favourite piece . . . the Bruch . . . '

'As I have already told you, *madame*, I have no son. I have my cottage here in the forest, my work, my dog and my donkey cart. I have the children who rely on me to make them happy each Noël. What more can a blind man without a memory desire?'

'Perhaps tomorrow, when we are gone, you might ask yourself that, Maxwell Barrett.' Lorna could not hide her anger and disappointment.

'Please go,' he said. 'And do not come back.'

'*Father!*' It was a cry from Simon's heart and the big man was not unmoved, for he blinked at the sound.

'I'll take you back to Mendibel,' he said gruffly, heading for the door.

Lorna Learns More

Zingaro loped ahead of them down the narrow, winding tracks. The dog was like a white ghost flitting here and there, but always running back to them, keeping them in sight.

'Is the boy all right?' Olentzero, up front, sat hunched over the reins of the donkey cart that he held loosely in his hands.

'He's asleep,' Lorna said, stroking Simon's head where it rested in her lap. 'He's exhausted.'

She waited, hoping that Max would engage her in conversation, but all he did was click his tongue and mutter encouraging words to Prunelle, his sweet-faced donkey with the soft brown coat and the mournful eyes.

The rain had stopped, finally, and the moon peeped from behind a silver-edged cloud, lighting up the sky and turning it from black to purple. A scattering of bright stars twinkled down on them and the Milky Way made a powdery trail across the Heavens.

'It's a beautiful night now,' Lorna said, because she could no longer stand the silence between them. 'The sky looks like sequinned velvet.'

She wanted to say how the sky reminded her of the dark blue evening dress she had worn to his first major concert. It was on the occasion when he had told her and the world that he was in love with her by dedicating the whole of the Bruch Violin Concerto to her. She had never felt so loved, nor so happy. Did he remember? Did he want to remember?

Lorna stared at the broad back and waited for a response, but none came. She saw him flex his shoulders slightly, but he remained silent until the dark silhouette of Mendibel appeared before them. Only one window had its shutters partly open, showing a yellow light spilling out on to the cobbled street.

The donkey drew to a halt as if bidden by a command that only it could hear. Even Zingaro came to stand close to Prunelle's shaggy sides, the pair of them as silent as the sleeping village.

'Is there a light?' Max asked.

'Yes,' Lorna told him.

'In that case I'll come no further,' he said. 'The light is coming from the home of Madame Lafon. She is waiting up for you.'

Lorna frowned. Somehow, she had to get through to him, but this was not the moment. Besides, there were things that could not be discussed in front of Simon. She would have to choose her moment and go to him. André Ducau would no doubt take her back to the house of Olentzero, if she asked him.

Simon stirred as she gently shook his shoulder. He sat up, rubbing his eyes and yawning. Then he remembered where he was and what had happened. He jumped from the cart and went to hold Prunelle's head, determined to speak to this man who was his father, but who insisted on denying it.

'Olentzero,' he announced in a clear voice full of determination. 'Can I come back to see you? Can I, please? You can show me how to carve the wood and I . . . I can play the violin for you. I wasn't very good today, but that was because I was nervous.'

Max raised one hand, halting the flow of the boy's words. He rubbed the hand over his face and gave an audible sigh.

'You must stay with your mother,' he said firmly. 'I have work to do and no time to be bothered by you.'

Simon's face crumpled and Lorna felt her own heart clench.

'If you really have lost your memory,' she said, 'how do you know that you are not the man we are looking for? How can you deny anything?'

'Please . . . no more!' Was that anguish she saw in those sightless eyes?

'How can you deny the son you always wanted, Max?'

He turned his head away from her.

'Don't you think I would know if I had a wife and a son? I am not the person you seek. That person no longer exists. Believe me.'

'You left me to go and entertain the troops, Max,' she continued, undaunted by his words. 'You said you would always love me, and you gave me the most precious gift.' She expected him to question her, but he simply sat, unmoving. 'The day I heard you were missing, I also discovered that I was to have your child. And here he is, Max. This is Simon, your son, and he is so like you it hurts every time I look at him.'

A sudden shudder seemed to take hold of Olentzero. He lifted the reins and called sharply to his dog. In seconds the cart was facing the way they had come.

'I must go,' he said, his voice as rough as the gravel kicked up by Prunelle's dainty hoofs.

'You should see him, Max,' Lorna shouted after him. 'You should get to know him. You would be so proud, so proud!'

But if he heard her, he made no sign.

* * *

She felt Simon standing close beside her and draped an arm about his shoulders, knowing that, like her, he was trying not to cry. A door clicked open behind them, but it wasn't the elderly Madame Lafon who appeared. Peering out into the night was Roberto's wife, Carla.

'*Olentzero!*' She ran out of the house, a blanket wrapped tightly about her slight form. '*Olentzero, c'est moi, Carla!*'

She ran swiftly past them without a glance. It did not take long for her to disappear from view as she followed the retreating donkey cart.

Lorna felt a stir of something unpleasant deep inside her. Bad enough that her own dearest husband should be in denial about his life before he crashed in the Iraty forests; but what was there going on between him and this young married Basque woman?

The expression on Carla's face had been unmistakably one of love.

'*Madame.*' Madame Lafon was now standing in her open doorway. '*Entrez! Entrez vite!*'

They entered the house. The warmth of the place after the intense damp cold of the air outside was more than welcome. The fire had been kept going and great pine logs were sending a sheet of flame and sparks flying up the chimney.

'*Regardez, madame,*' the old lady said, indicating a figure in the corner of the room; a familiar figure that rose stiffly and stepped forward to take her in his protective arms.

'David! You're back!' Lorna sank against him, then drew back and looked at the man she had been on the verge of marrying until a very few hours ago. 'But what have you done to yourself?'

'Sorry about this,' David said, smiling

sheepishly. 'I fell down a mountain, well, down one of the mountain slopes. I'm a bit bruised and battered, I'm afraid, and I broke my wrist. But it's my pride that took the biggest beating.'

He had cuts and bruises on his face and a yellowing black eye. And one arm was in a plaster cast from elbow to fingers.

'Oh, you poor thing!'

'Fortunately, it's the right arm that's broken, so I was able to drive, with difficulty.' When he grinned he looked like a little boy in need of a hug, and yet Lorna found she could not, after that first rush of relief at seeing him, bring herself to touch him.

'You shouldn't have driven,' she said. 'You could have phoned, once the phone lines were repaired.'

'I had to get back to you, Lorna,' David said, limping back to his chair and sitting down carefully. 'I met Roberto in the hospital. He told me what happened.'

'Poor Roberto. How is he?'

'He told me to tell you not to worry. They're keeping him in for a couple of days, just in case.'

Simon, who had been almost asleep on his feet, suddenly pushed forward and placed himself between David and his mother.

'You can't marry my mum now,' he said. 'You see, we found my *real* dad. He's Olentzero!'

★   ★   ★

Madame Lafon bustled about the room putting plates of fish soup on the table, muttering crossly to herself. Every now and then, Lorna made out the names, 'Carla' and 'Olentzero'. There was definitely something going on between those two that the old lady did not approve of.

'Lorna, is this true, what Simon is saying?' David looked at her expectantly, his eyes already registering a hint of wretchedness. 'Simon says that this man, Olentzero, is his father. What kind of ridiculous thing is that!' He gave a mocking, but nervous, laugh.

Lorna drew in a long breath and put her hand over her mouth to hide the fact that her lips were quivering.

Ever since they had arrived in Mendibel nothing had seemed real. She suspected that nothing would ever be real again.

'Simon, I have to keep pinching myself to prove that I'm not living some kind of weird dream,' she said, then, slowly and carefully, she recounted the story of what had happened from the moment David had left to go skiing.

'And you really think that this fellow, Olentzero, is your long-lost husband?' David looked as confused as she felt.

'I know he is, David,' Lorna said, allowing Madam Lafon to push her into a chair and place a large soup spoon in her hand, with urgent mutterings to make her eat. 'There's no mistake. It's Max all right.'

Simon was getting the same treatment from Madame Lafon as she had given to Lorna, but when he gripped the spoon, he did not eat with it; he banged it on the table.

'Why doesn't he want to know us?' he cried, his cheeks flaming crimson and his eyes awash with tears. 'I haven't done anything wrong. Why does he hate me?'

Lorna could see how her son was suffering, though he would never know the pain she herself carried, and had carried for so long in her heart, since Max's disappearance.

'He doesn't hate you, Simon,' she said. 'How could he? He didn't even know that you had been born.'

'But I don't understand!'

'Simon, I don't understand, either. All I can promise you, is that I'll try to work it out, try to . . . '

'No! You're not trying to do that at all. You'd rather marry David.'

With that, he threw down his spoon and ran from the table, upsetting his chair in the process. David picked up the chair, under the critical gaze of

Madam Lafon, who gave a grunt and placed a large *roule* of bread on the table, with another order to them to, '*mangez!*'

'Do you think you should go to him?' David said.

'Max?' Lorna asked. 'Or Simon?'

'Perhaps you need to go to both.'

★   ★   ★

Just for a moment, Lorna felt overwhelmed with love for this man who had been a part of her life for so long. Yet it was Max who still occupied the greater part of her heart. Max, who was still alive.

'Oh, David, I don't know what to do,' she said to the cooling bowl of fish soup, because she could not bring herself to meet his gaze.

'Nobody can tell you what to do, Lorna,' David said. 'You must do what is best for you and your son. Whatever you decide . . . well, I'll always be here for you. I'll always be your friend.'

Lorna's throat was so tight she could not utter a word. She simply gave him a watery smile, then reached out and squeezed his hand. Poor David. He hadn't asked be a part of all this. He could have walked away, but would never do anything like that. He was her prop and she needed his support now more than ever before, selfish though that seemed.

★   ★   ★

I'll always be your friend. That's what David had said. Lorna finally drifted off to sleep hours later with his words ringing in her ears along with Max's, *I have no wife. No son!*

It seemed as if she was awake every few minutes, tossing and turning, praying for the strength to deal with this complicated state of affairs, not only for herself, but for Simon. And for Max and David, too. It also appeared, however, that whatever she did, someone would get hurt. The most important person in the equation, however, was her son. To secure his happiness she was prepared to make any sacrifice.

★　★　★

As the morning rays of light caressed the land, with its twittering birdsong and the loud crowing of a proud rooster, Lorna opened her eyes and found herself full of resolve. There was no getting away from the fact that she had never stopped loving Max.

'Simon!' She touched the boy gently and he opened his eyes, blinking up at her hazily at first, then growing immediately alert.

'Get up and get dressed, Simon. Quickly.'

'Why?' The question was automatic, even though he had swung his legs out of bed before uttering the word.

'This is something we've got to do together,' she told him as she scrubbed at herself with cold water. 'We can't just turn our backs on your father. We owe it to him to try to bring his memory back to life.'

'But he won't remember me,' Simon said, washing his face and little else, using only the tips of his fingers and hopping from one foot to the other as the icy water hit him.

Lorna hurriedly got dressed. 'Your father and I had such a happy life together before the war came along. Maybe we can get some of that memory back and then . . . well, we'll see.'

'How are we going to do that?' Simon's eyes grew large and round.

'I wish I knew, Simon, but hopefully, I'll think of something. Come on. Are you ready?'

He nodded enthusiastically and threw his arms about his mother, hugging her tightly for the briefest moments.

'Thank you, Mum!'

Downstairs, she could hear Roberto's mother rattling crockery and there was the usual aroma of freshly baked bread infiltrating the single layer of timbers that separated the ground floor from the floor above.

The old woman had been up and working since five. Lorna had laid awake, counting the chimes of the clock in the hall. And in between the hours, she had listened to the hollow tick-tock of every second going by.

There was also a murmur of voices and since they were either speaking in the patios of the Pyrenees or the even more complicated Basque, it was not David down there. He had been very tired last night and Madame Lafon had made up a bed for him in a box room, refusing to hear of him returning to St Jean de Pied Port at such a late hour, considering the sorry state he was in.

★   ★   ★

The person talking with Madame Lafon was André Ducau. As Lorna entered the warm kitchen, he was already sitting at the table, tearing chunks of still-warm bread from a

195

family-sized loaf and drinking steaming *café au lait* from the traditional drinking bowl. He gave her a broad smile of welcome.

'Bonjour, madame! You are well?'

'I'm very well, thank you, André,' she said, and nodded her thanks to Madam Lafon, who quickly laid another two places at the table. 'I'm glad you are here. I need to talk to you about . . . about Olentzero.'

'He is very good man, madame, but he does not like people to intrude in his life. He is very private person.'

'But that's just it, André. The man you know as Olentzero is actually my husband. For years I thought he was dead. He is Simon's father, and until yesterday they had never met.'

André stared down into his bowl of coffee, slowly tearing off more bread and dipping it into the steaming liquid.

'Madame Barrett,' he said. 'There are only one or two of us who know that this man is not the real Olentzero. He is an Englishman who came down in his

196

plane during the war. He has no memory, other than his time spent at the side of the great Olentzero. I was with Roberto the day of the crash. Carla too. We were very young, you understand, but we knew all about the dangers of war.'

'There were Germans in our village. Little by little, we hid the plane and buried the men . . . the dead ones. The Englishman who survived did not have any identification. It was lost in the crash. He was terribly hurt. We could not let him fall into the hands of the Gestapo. We left him in the hands of Olentzero, with Carla to help care for him.'

'Carla! But she must have been very young at the time.'

'We have the same age, Carla and me,' André said, nodding his head slowly. 'But in time of war, *madame*, one does not remain a child for long. Carla was very beautiful. The German soldiers . . . Roberto was taking her to Olentzero for protection when the plane came down. There was much confusion.'

'And later?' Lorna had to put to André the questions that were battering at her brain. 'Carla stayed with Olentzero . . . and the Englishman?'

'Yes. Her child was born up there in Olentzero's little house. She did not come back to the village until the Germans had left. It was difficult for her, but Roberto married her and the people did not speak of this again.'

'André,' Lorna traced a line in the grain of the old wooden table with a finger that shook slightly. 'Last night, when Olentzero brought Simon and me back here, Carla ran after him. Why would she do that, do you think?'

She saw the young man's cheek muscles tense. He dropped his gaze and spoke almost in a mumble.

'Because she is in love with the Englishman who fell from the sky. She is married to Roberto, a good man, but . . . ach, that Carla! She is obsessed with the man we know as Olentzero.'

A Visit To The Forest

Lorna's blood turned to ice and her heart plummeted. Carla might be volatile and jealous, but there was no denying how beautiful she was. Any man would find it difficult to turn away if she were to throw herself at him. Certainly, a man without a past, lost and alone in an alien world, would be hard put to refuse her attentions. Whether Max remembered anything at all about his previous life, his denial could well be because of Carla.

'Poor Roberto,' she said softly, then saw André's stricken face and guessed that there was much more to the story. 'André, were you in love with Carla?'

He turned away to stare out of the window, where the light was gilding the trees and a robin trilled before dropping on to the windowsill looking for crumbs.

'I thought it was an Englishman who . . . ?' Lorna couldn't finish the sentence. What if that Englishman had been Max!

'Ah, *oui*! It was an Englishman who is the father of Carla's child. But that was before the Germans arrived in Mendibel.'

'Oh, I see . . . ' The relief Lorna felt was immense.

André threw his hands in the air. 'What does it matter now? I never stood a chance with Carla. She still sees me as '*petit André*', the friend of her childhood.' He heaved a great sigh. 'Besides, it is Olentzero she loves, even though she is married to Roberto, who will always look after her.'

'And Max . . . I mean, Olentzero . . . ? Does he . . . ?' Lorna held her breath, dreading his answer.

'Olentzero is a good, wise man,' André said. 'He is gentle with Carla. He understands her problems and he lets her talk about them. He is the only man she really trusts. But no, there is no love on his part.'

'You're a very nice person, André,' Lorna told him. 'One day you'll meet someone and be happy.'

He slowly shook his head. 'No, I think not. I will become a hermit, like Olentzero. Perhaps, one day, I will be Olentzero.'

Lorna went to him, resting her hand lightly on his shoulder.

'I'm so sorry, André.'

'And I am sad for you, and for the boy.'

★　★　★

They were sitting in mutual silence when Simon rushcd into the room, pulled his chair out from the table with a noisy flourish and grabbed unceremoniously for the bread and the jam. Madame Lafon immediately came forward with a pan of warmed milk and poured some into a drinking bowl. Simon thanked her, his mouth already full, and she patted his head affectionately.

'Have you asked him, Mum?' Simon said. 'Is André going to take us back to see Olentzero?'

André's chin jerked up and a deep frown furrowed his brow. Lorna gave him an apologetic look. 'I was going to ask you to take us back into the forest.'

'I cannot do that, Madame Barrett,' André said, his eyes troubled as he looked from Lorna to Simon and back again.

'Why can't you?' Simon looked up from his drinking bowl and stared at them both.

'Because . . . ' André spread his hands in a hopeless gesture. 'I must respect the wishes of Olentzero.'

'In that case,' Simon said, reaching for a second piece of bread, 'I'll just have to find my father myself. I did it yesterday, didn't I?'

'If I remember rightly, young man,' Lorna said, doing her best to keep her words light, 'you were good and lost.'

There was a quick exchange of words in Basque between André and Madame

Lafon, who did a lot of head shaking and tutting and sucking in of air through her teeth. Then her hands, too, were thrown in the air and she took herself off to feed the chickens and geese in the yard at the back of the house.

'What was all that about?' Lorna asked, in no doubt that the heated discussion had had something to do with her and Olentzero.

'She does not approve of Carla,' André said. 'She says she was wrong last night to run after Olentzero. But most of all, she does not like it that Carla is married to Roberto.'

'I think I can understand that,' Lorna said, and looked at Simon with a sigh. 'Well, Simon, when you've finished your breakfast, shall we go?'

'Are we really going to see my father again?' Simon brightened immediately. 'Really, Mum?'

'We can try,' she told him. 'I'll just tell David . . . '

'No need,' David's voice behind her

made her jump. 'Let me come with you, Lorna. I would hate to think of the pair of you getting lost in the forest.'

'It's all right.' André was reaching for his beret and sheepskin jacket as he spoke. 'I am a good guide. And only Roberto and I know how to find Olentzero.'

'Thank you, André,' Lorna said.

'No problem. It's right that I do this.'

'All right,' David said, giving a pained smile, 'but I'd like to come with you.'

'David . . . why?' Lorna asked.

'Let's say I have a vested interest in the outcome of this visit,' he said. 'There are things to be settled between you and Max . . . and between you and me. The sooner we get it over with, the better.'

'Yes, of course. I owe you that much.' Lorna said, ignoring Simon's thunderous expression.

'We go now, please!' André ordered, heading for the door, with a shouted explanation for their departure to Madame Lafon in the yard outside.

'Today, the weather, it is better. No storms, but very cold.'

★ ★ ★

It was just as André had said. The walk would have been very pleasant had it not been for the fact that they were all so tense. David walked in silence for the most part, bringing up the rear. Simon kept close to his mother, and Lorna was surprised that he did not characteristically run on ahead. André strode out, taking the lead, and from time to time he turned and waited for them to catch up.

'It's that way,' Simon said at one point, but was immediately corrected by André. 'Well, I thought it was that way.'

'There are probably several routes to take,' Lorna said gently. 'But I think it's best to leave it up to André.'

'I don't see why David has to come,' Simon said in a whisper.

Lorna gave her son a hug. 'I'm sure he just wants to protect us.'

⋆　⋆　⋆

The going was beginning to get tough. The recent rain had turned the ground into a quagmire. But despite the mud, it didn't seem to take quite so long to find what they were looking for. When a thin whorl of grey wood smoke drifting above the tree lined announced the approach of Olentzero's cottage, Lorna felt a nervous stirring in her stomach. In a few minutes she would again be face to face with her husband. And again she would be fighting the urge to cling desperately to him.

'Almost there,' she said breathlessly to David, who stared ahead with narrowed eyes and drawn-in cheeks. He grabbed her wrist suddenly, halting her in her tracks. His good hand went to touch her cheek and his smile wavered uneasily.

'Lorna . . . '

'Yes, David?'

'I just want you to know. I do love you, and I want to marry you . . . '

'But I'm already married, David,' she said, her voice faltering. 'Max is still alive, even though he doesn't seem to remember me or our life together. But as long as there's a chance . . . I owe it to him to . . . to stick by him. Oh, David, I loved him so much! I still do.'

'What if this visit doesn't work out? What if he refuses to acknowledge you and Simon? Will you still love him, Lorna? Can you really stand there and tell me that our relationship is over?'

'I don't know what to say, David,' she told him, which was as honest as she could be right at that moment.

'Lorna,' he said, gripping her shoulder, 'I'll wait for you, as long as it takes, if there's any chance that you could spend the rest of your life with me. You, and Simon. I'll do whatever it takes to make you both happy. You must believe that.'

Lorna felt a lump growing in her constricted throat. She planted a light kiss on his cold cheek. 'Yes, David,' she said. 'I do believe that, really I do. But I need time . . . we all need time . . . '

She saw him begin to nod, start to say something else, but there was a distracting cry from the ridge above them. Lorna looked up to see André and Simon standing on the highest rise of ground a few hundred yards away, both of them waving impatiently.

Without a further word, Lorna and David plodded up the hillside, stepping over sodden, tangled fronds of bracken and dodging the low pine branches that dripped rainwater like showers of liquid diamonds.

And suddenly there was the cottage, just as she remembered it, nestling in a deep hollow. It was surrounded by a blanket of emerald green moss, butcher's broom, and holly that was full of the red berries of winter. There was a small figure hunched on the doorstep and even at that distance, there was no mistaking Carla. Her weeping seemed to fill the very air.

'Good Heavens!' David slithered to a

stop beside Lorna. 'What's up with that girl? Is she hurt?'

André came to the open cottage doorway and beckoned frantically. 'Come!' he cried out urgently. 'Come! There is trouble!'

★ ★ ★

They ran, as best they could, down to the cottage over the rough ground. Lorna's heart was pounding in fearful anticipation. There was no sign of Olentzero. Had there been an accident? What awful thing had happened? Don't let Max be dead, she prayed. *Not now. Not when I've found him again.*

Her fears were not entirely ground-less. Lorna allowed herself sufficient time to give a curious glance at Carla, but the young woman did not look up. She kept her head buried and went on weeping hysterically. It was comforting to Lorna to feel David press closely behind her, his hand protectively at her back.

'Come!' André called from the dim interior, and as they entered, moving into the one big living space, the sunlight fell across the figure of Olentzero sitting, slightly slumped, at the table in the centre of the room. 'He is hurt.'

Olentzero, or Max — Lorna no longer knew what to call him — was clutching a bloodstained towel to a wound in his chest.

Lorna gave a stifled cry and rushed forward, but was stopped short when Olentzero lifted his head and waved a hand vaguely in her direction.

'It's nothing!' he said, his voice ragged, his face ashen with pain. 'I'm all right.'

'You're anything but all right,' Lorna said, and this time he allowed her to pull his hand away and lift the towel. 'Who did this to you?'

'It was Carla,' André said, coming forward with some clean cloth that he was tearing up into strips.

'Carla! But what made her do such a

thing?' Lorna cleaned the wound as best she could, relieved that it was not as serious as she had first thought.

'Don't be too hard on the girl,' Olentzero said. 'She didn't mean to kill me, otherwise she would have chosen her weapon more wisely.' He indicated the chisel that lay on the table beside him.

'The girl is dangerous,' David said.

'She is unhappy,' Olentzero said. 'She made the mistake of thinking that I somehow belonged to her. Today I had to tell her that she was wrong.'

'But still . . . ' David persisted.

'Don't be too hard on her.' A pair of bright blue eyes shone out of a weathered face. 'Her mind is damaged because of what happened to her during the war. Roberto tried to put things right. He did a good job, but it wasn't enough.'

'How sad,' Lorna murmured, and turned for the door, meaning to go and comfort the girl, but Carla jumped to her feet and ran deep into the forest.

'I will go to her,' André said, and before anyone could stop him, he was running after her.

★ ★ ★

Lorna saw the way that David was look-ing at Olentzero, and Simon was watching the two of them even more closely.

'Max . . . ' She quickly corrected herself. 'Olentzero, if you prefer. This is David. We've been . . . friends . . . for a long time.'

'Why have you come back here?' Olentzero demanded.

Lorna tried desperately to think of the right thing to say, but knew that nothing she said would make any impact if he were truly suffering from amnesia. So delving into her backpack, she drew out a photograph and placed it on the table.

'Perhaps this will mean something to you.'

His fingers crept out, found the photograph, and pushed it away from him. 'Why do you show a photograph to a blind man?'

'Anyone who looks at it will tell you that it's a photograph of you, Max,' she told him softly. 'Without the beard, of course.'

He made a deprecating sound and turned away from her, but Simon grabbed the photograph and pushed it back into his father's hands.

'It's true! It's you and Mum . . . ' A sob rose in his throat.

'Look here, Max or Olentzero, or whatever your name is,' David, said, 'I stand to lose an awful lot if you are who Lorna claims you are. But believe me, though it pains me to say this, she's right. The man in this photograph is undoubtedly you, and Lorna is standing beside you. The pair of you look so happy on your wedding day that it hurts me to look at it.'

'The man in that photograph is dead. So why don't you take her away from here and make her and the boy happy?'

'Don't you think that's exactly what I

would like to do?'

'So?'

'I'd be a fool to believe that Lorna could ever be happy with anybody but Maxwell Barrett. As long as she knows you're alive, nobody else stands a chance with her.'

'I've never heard of Maxwell Barrett.' Olentzero pushed his chair back and stood up. 'Now, please go. I have work to do.'

'You're hurt, man!'

'The wound is not deep. It will heal.'

Simon, as they were talking, had been gathering up an armful of half-finished carvings of miniature violins.

'You did these,' he said, throwing them down on the table. 'You make violins. My father used to make violins. And you look just like him, and I'm not leaving here until you stop lying to me and my mother.'

There was a short, stunned silence and Olentzero ran a less than steady hand across his face.

'I'm not lying, son,' he said, and turned to face the fire that was crackling in the chimney. 'Now, all of you, please go and leave me in peace!'

'Come on, Lorna,' David said, putting an arm gently about her and drawing her towards the door. 'Simon . . . ?'

'I'm not coming!'

Simon was determinedly standing his ground. In his hands he had his father's violin, which he raised to his chin, He took a deep breath and drew the bow across the strings. The air became electric as the child struggled through the piece that he had spent so long learning.

'No, no, no!' Olentzero's head shot up as he beat a fist on the high mantelshelf, making the few items arranged there dance with the impact. 'It sounds like you are strangling a cat! Bruch must be played with tenderness . . . with passion. Where's your emotion, boy? Start again.'

They heard Simon's sobs before they erupted in a cry, exultant and heartbreaking at the same time.

'I can't!' he said. 'You're the great Olentzero! You show me! Show me . . . please!'

It seemed like they were all fixed in time, unable to speak, unable to move. Olentzero turned to look in Simon's direction. He held out his hands and the boy placed the violin in them. Then he raised the instrument to his shoulder. Lorna held her breath as the other arm raised the bow, which hovered over the violin, trembling like a branch in the wind.

The bow never made it to the strings. They all heard his gasp just before he threw the violin down with a snort of disgust. Lorna's heart sank, not only for herself, but for Max, and especially for their son.

'What am I doing?' Max said gruffly. 'I'm a carpenter, not a violinist. I make charcoal for a living and carve Christmas presents for children. Music is not part of my life.'

Lorna felt like beating her fists on the chest of the husband who refused to admit who he really was. 'The great Olentzero has his priorities and they are not the same as the great, much-loved, much missed Maxwell Barrett. Olentzero makes toys for the village children, who are more important to him than his own son, whose hopes he prefers to destroy!'

The silence that followed Lorna's outburst wrapped around them like a smothering blanket.

'Oh, Mum!' Simon's face puckered and he ran to her, his face awash with tears.

'Come on, sweetheart,' she said, pressing her lips to his head. 'Monsieur Olentzero doesn't want us here, spoiling things for him.'

David Decides To Act

Bad weather arrived in the form of a few flakes of snow floating down from the high peaks as they reached the valley. By the time they reached the village, the flakes were thicker, and the trees behind them were already coated in snow. Soon, the landscape seemed to fade into a blur behind a great curtain of dazzling white lace.

'Roberto tells me it's possible to ski around here if the snow is thick enough,' David said, as they stood in the hallway of the Lafon house, brushing flakes and melting ice from their shoulders.

He looked from Lorna to Simon, but neither of them was showing any interest in his attempt to take their mind off the experience they had just shared. Simon raced upstairs with heavy feet and the house shook as he slammed the bedroom door.

Lorna heaved a great sigh and headed for the living room, where she could already hear the fire crackling in the grate and feel its welcoming warmth. Perhaps she ought to have gone after Simon, but she did not feel able to face her young son at that moment. First she had to get her own emotions under control. Simon had never seen her cry. She would prefer it if he never did.

Madame Lafon bustled out of the room, rosy-cheeked and cheerful, as Lorna and David entered, muttering something about making them a hot *tisane*. Her *tisanes* were strange, herbal concoctions that had a surprisingly relaxing effect. Quite the opposite to her *café*, which was black and strong and almost unpalatable.

'Lorna . . . ' David said, pulling her around to face him, 'Lorna, I don't know what to say, except that I'm terribly sorry things have worked out . . . well, badly, I suppose . . . for you and Simon.'

Lorna pushed her anger and disappointment away and tried to act reasonably. Maybe on the surface it worked, but underneath she was hurting as much as a young girl mourning the loss of her first love. And, indeed, Max had been just that. Her first, her *only* love.

'Thank you, David, for being there for us,' she said.

A sound behind them made them both jump as they realised they were not alone in the room.

'I am so sorry,' Roberto Lafon said, as he struggled painfully out of the low, sagging sofa where he had been lying, hidden from view. 'I did not mean to startle you.'

'Roberto! I thought you were in hospital! What are you doing back here?'

'They speak of much snow on the way. I did not wish to be stranded in the town, so I persuaded them to discharge me.' He tilted his head to one side and smiled at them. 'Don't worry. I am all right. But you ... *chère madame* ... I see great sadness in your eyes. The visit with Olentzero did not go well?'

Lorna shook her head, unable to trust her voice to reply to him. He limped across the floor and took both her hands in his, which brought her so close to tears she quickly withdrew them with a watery smile. She went to warm herself at the fire. It allowed her time to recover her composure.

'The man's a fool,' David said, sitting down heavily. 'He stood there and lied to us. He knows who he is, all right. This business of amnesia and refusal to admit that he's not Maxwell Barrett ... well, it just doesn't ring true to me.'

'Oh, *mes amies*, but it *is* true. The Englishman had nothing when we found him. No clothes, no memory. Of that we were all convinced. He did not speak a word for months.'

'But he does remember now,' David maintained. 'For instance, he knew that piece of music young Simon played for him. And he criticised the poor lad's playing.'

'*Mais oui*. Gradually, he fits together small pieces of his past. They come to him like . . . how do you say . . . flashes? But there are large holes in his memory. It is a frightening place to be, you know, when you do not have a past.'

'Did he . . . ?' Lorna gave a gulp and struggled to carry on. 'Did he know he was married, Roberto? He couldn't have known that he had a son, but surely . . . did he ever remember *me?*'

Roberto shook his head and eased himself back carefully on to the sofa. 'He told me that he was sure there had been someone in his life, but he could not bring her face or her voice to mind. He knew his parents were dead and that there were no brothers or sisters, so he felt he had nothing to go back to England for.'

'Nothing to go back for!' Lorna's fists clenched.

'Steady, darling,' David said.

Steady! She thought, under the

circumstances, that she was being amazingly steady. Here she was in France, thinking she was here to establish once and for all that her husband had died in a plane crash more than a decade ago, and he had turned out to be still alive. And he showed no inclination to have anything to do with her. Worst of all, he had rejected his son. Yes, she was incredibly steady, in the circumstances.

'Is his refusal to accept me anything to do with Carla?' She couldn't help herself asking the question.

'My wife thinks she is in love with Olentzero . . . ' Roberto spread his hands and gave a grimacing smile. 'I am sorry, but we have never known him by any other name. It is sad, *non?* I love Carla, who loves another, and he . . . '

'He?' Lorna arched her eyebrows at him and waited.

'If he loves anyone,' Roberto said, 'it is not Carla.'

★   ★   ★

223

The snow fell thicker and thicker, with blizzards that took away visibility and built high, white walls that blocked the roads and tracks for miles around. Whether they wanted to or not, the English visitors to the little village of Mendibel were obliged to stay.

Simon would be reluctant to leave, in any case. As long as he could stay here, he could dream that his father would one day come for him. David, on the other hand, would rejoice as soon as they could head back home.

As for Lorna, a lot of the time she felt bereft of feelings. Her emotions were locked away somewhere deep inside her. Perhaps, once she got away from Iraty and Max, she would see things more clearly.

Carla returned, briefly, and announced that she would be spending Noël at a friend's house at the other side of the village. Roberto seemed to accept the situation with well-practised resignation. Mixel seized the opportunity to have a little independence away from his mother.

It was also good news to Mixel and Joseba that Simon would be staying. The three boys had bonded well. It was something Lorna was grateful for. At least, while Simon was with them, it occupied his mind with things other than his reluctant father.

★　★　★

'If only we had been able to go back to England,' Lorna said to David, as they were looking out at a totally white world a few days later. 'It would have given Simon a chance to forget what happened with Max.'

'Perhaps, but there doesn't appear to be a choice,' David said.

'It looks like we'll be spending Christmas here after all,' Lorna said with a heavy sigh. 'And I haven't got a present for Simon . . . or you.'

He smiled tenderly and she saw the love in his eyes. This was so unfair on all of them, but particularly on David, who had been so generous in bringing them here in the first place. All this business with Max must be tearing him apart. Any other man would have stormed off long ago.

'Not to worry, love,' he said now. 'We have each other . . . don't we?'

Lorna found she couldn't hold his gaze. She turned and stared back through the window at the white-blanketed slopes, in the direction of the track that led to the charcoal maker's cottage, the legendary Olentzero . . . and Max. She drew in a deep breath. 'I'm so glad that Roberto invited us to stay in the schoolhouse with him,' she said. 'It was beginning to get claustrophobic in old Madame Lafon's house. I doubt if Carla likes the arrangement, though.'

Lorna frowned at her reflection in the darkening windowpane as the sun set over the blurred smudges of firs that made up the bulk of the Iraty forest. Which was where her love lay, she thought. Where she should be, her and Simon.

Oh, Max! We were so much in love, my darling. Why are you doing this? What can I say or do to make everything right for us all?

'Are you all right, Lorna?' She hadn't noticed that David had come to stand beside her.

'It's nothing. Don't worry about me, David. It's Simon who concerns me. He's so young. How can he possibly be expected to sort out all this in his mind? I barely understand it myself.'

'I know, I know.'

★ ★ ★

David was being so considerate, despite all that was going on in his own heart. Perhaps she should have married him long ago, Lorna thought. She could have done that. She *should* have done that. Stringing him along had been cruel.

'David,' she said now, touching his cheek, 'if you want to leave me . . . I mean, leave me for good, I'll understand. Honestly I will. I should never have allowed you to get so involved.'

'Nonsense. I brought you here because I knew I didn't stand a chance unless you could draw a definite line between the past with Max and a future with me.'

'You know, David,' she said huskily, 'I really don't deserve you.'

'That's funny,' he said, with a smile that squeezed her heart. 'That's exactly what I think. I always thought you were far too good for me.'

His smile was cheerless, not reaching his eyes, which were clouded with sadness. He picked up her hand and kissed the backs of her fingers. It made her heart break. She was caught between two men she loved dearly. David, whom she could have and who would be a good husband and father . . . and Max, whom she had loved and lost, and was now trying desperately to hate, but failing miserably.

'I'm going to talk to Roberto about the weather,' David said, heading for the hall. 'Unfortunately, I don't think any of us will be able to leave just yet. The snow just keeps on falling and building up in horrendous drifts. I can't see it clearing before Christmas.'

That thought filled Lorna with mixed feelings. Part of her wished she could be a million miles away, wished she had never given in to Simon's pleading to search for Max.

If only she could reach out to him, get through the fog that was swirling around his brain. But she was lost for ideas. How could they begin to find again the love they had once shared?

★   ★   ★

How long she sat there in the schoolhouse, staring into the fire, mulling things over and over in her mind, she did not know. The wood burned to an ashy glow and she shivered in the lowering temperature. She threw another log on the fire and sank back against the cushions.

A few minutes later, a clatter of feet

in the hall and a cacophony of excited young voices jolted her out of a light slumber. She sat up just as Simon and his two Basque pals, Mixel and Joseba, burst enthusiastically into the room. They were covered in snow, which immediately started to melt all over the floor, droplets hissing in the flames as they shook themselves close to the fire.

'Goodness, what have you three been up to?' Lorna couldn't help smiling at Simon's bright eyes and rosy cheeks.

'We went tobogganing,' Simon said breathlessly. 'It was super, Mum. You should see the snow. It's this deep.'

He indicated a height way above his head. Mixel pulled his hand down a few inches and Joseba pulled it even further, then all three of them nodded in agreement.

'Deep, anyway,' Simon grinned.

'You stay now for Noël,' Mixel said earnestly. 'That is so, eh, *monsieur*?'

David had reappeared and was surveying the happy boys. 'I've been speaking to Roberto and André,' he said. 'They say there's no chance of getting through to St Jean Pied de Port, or anywhere else, for that matter. All the roads and passes for miles around are totally blocked. It hasn't snowed like this for years, apparently.'

'That sounds ominous,' Lorna said. 'I hope the villagers have enough food stocks to last out.'

'I don't think we need worry on that score.' David sat down beside her and gave her a reassuring hug. 'But we're here for Christmas all right. And maybe even the New Year.'

'I'm all lost with the days,' Lorna said, shaking her head in confusion. 'When is Christmas Eve?'

'It's in two days,' David told her and their eyes locked as the same thought went through their heads.

'*Noël!*' shouted Joseba. 'That is when Olentzero comes into the village with his donkey and cart! He brings us the toys he has made!'

'Perhaps he will bring a gift for you, too, Simon,' said Mixel.

Simon's face seemed to reflect every emotion possible at hearing Joseba and Mixel's words. His smile transformed itself into a quivering struggle between laughter and tears. It was laced with so much hope that Lorna wanted to take him in her arms and cuddle him like she had done when he was a baby. She wanted so much to make it all right for him.

'There is a problem?' Mixel could tell that Simon was troubled about something.

'No!' Simon said with a brave but wobbly grin. 'It's great! Isn't it, Mum? Isn't it, David?'

'That's wonderful, Simon,' David said, with a slightly anxious look that mirrored Lorna's thoughts.

Please let there be a present for Simon.

★   ★   ★

Later, when the boys had gone back out into the snow and Lorna was left alone with David, she voiced her anxiety. 'Oh,

David, what if he doesn't have anything for Simon?' she said, not looking at him because she could no longer bear the hurt in his eyes. 'He would be so humiliated in front of all his new friends. Finding out that he is the son of Olentzero has been something of a bonus to him.'

'Yes,' David said. 'I've noticed how the children of the village seem to treat him like a young hero.'

'It's all going to go wrong,' Lorna sighed, 'I can feel it. Simon will be so hurt and, worst of all, he'll never forgive Max.'

'That blasted husband of yours!' David's anger burst out. 'I've a good mind to . . . '

'Stop it, David,' Lorna said. 'We don't know what Max has been through. How can we begin to understand what it was like for him to be hurt and have no memory in a foreign country teeming with enemy soldiers?'

David shook his head despairingly. 'I still say the man's a fool. I saw the way he looked every time you spoke. It shook him to the very marrow. He remembers you all right. I'd like to know what game he's playing.'

It was true. Lorna had seen how Max had flinched visibly the first time he heard her voice, and again, later, when she had pleaded with him. A strange, haunted expression had gripped him. She wasn't convinced that he remembered everything, but something had jolted his memory. Maybe that something would remain there, nagging at him, until one day everything would start flooding back.

'Maybe . . . ' she began to speak, but David threw up his hands and marched to the door.

'I'm sorry, Lorna,' he said on his way out, 'but I can't stand any more of this.'

'What are you going to do?'

'I don't know. Something. We just can't leave things as they are. The slate will never be wiped clean. Not as long as Maxwell Barrett is on this earth.'

'David!' Lorna called out after him,

but he had gone.

She sat alone, frowning down at her hands lying helplessly in her lap. She hoped that David was not going to do something they would all regret.

Christmas Eve

The days and hours leading up to Christmas Eve stretched before Lorna like a yawning chasm, every minute taking longer and longer to tick by. And if it was bad for her, she could well imagine what it was like for Simon. Her son, bless him, did his best to hide his anxiety from her. His smile, though, was decidedly wobbly and he spent a lot of time staring blankly out of the window. Wishing and waiting. Perhaps for the impossible.

David was putting on a good show of being relaxed, either chatting to Roberto over a game of chess, or sitting with his nose buried in a book. However, he sometimes got up abruptly and left the room, a deep frown creasing his forehead. Once or twice he wrapped up warmly and went out into the vast winter wonderland, sometimes staying out long enough to make Lorna worry about his safety.

'Where does he go, Roberto?' she asked.

Roberto got up stiffly and limped across the room to peer out at the darkening landscape. 'Do you speak of David?' he said, giving her a quick look over his shoulder before resuming his vigil through the small glass panes of the window.

'Yes. He's so restless. I know he talks to you, Roberto, but I can't follow too well when you speak in rapid French.'

'He is a good man, your David,' Roberto said. 'He loves you very much.'

'Yes, I know, and that's why I feel so guilty.'

'Guilty?' Roberto turned. 'Because you don't love him the way he loves you?'

Lorna hesitated. Were her feelings so transparent?

'Perhaps,' she said.

'You are still obsessed by the man you married, I am thinking. The man you say is our Olentzero.'

'Olentzero or Max . . . ' Her eyes filled with unexpected tears. 'They are one and the same. And I can't believe that he remembers nothing, feels nothing.'

Roberto rested his hand on her shoulder, his eyes dull with sadness.

'When we found him, he was almost dead,' he told her. 'We had to hide him, care for him in secret. You have no idea what life was like for us here during the war. The forests were running with Nazis. If they had found him, they would have shot him as a spy, for he had no uniform, no identification. They would have killed everyone in this village, women and children included.'

'For a very long time, the English-man had no memory. The amnesia was genuine, of that I am sure. Later, I think perhaps that some things came back to him, but he would never speak of his past. He simply ignored our questions, so we learned that above all he valued his privacy. We respected his wishes.'

'But surely the British government must have asked questions?' Lorna said. 'He was an officer in the Royal Air Force, after all.'

Roberto shuffled painfully back to his place on the sofa. 'They did not know where his plane was. He was just one of the many missing in action. In fact, he was safe for some years, until that piece of his plane turned up recently. I was with a party of tourists when we stumbled across it, otherwise I would not have reported the find. Officials came out from England then and asked questions.'

'They dug around, but of course there was nothing. I'm afraid they just assumed that all the crew had perished at the time of impact. One can hardly blame them.'

'No,' Lorna sighed, 'I suppose not. And if Max, for whatever reason, didn't want to be found . . . '

The sound of the front door opening

made them both start. There were heavy footsteps and a low murmur of male voices. Lorna looked up expectantly as David, followed by André, entered the room, shaking off snowflakes and water droplets as they crossed to warm themselves in front of the fire. Both men had an air of secrecy about them that bothered her.

'You've been a long time,' she said to David's back. 'Where did you go?'

David straightened slightly, but continued to hold out his cold hands to the flames. André was looking at him, carefully avoiding Lorna's questioning gaze.

'André's been teaching me how to use snow shoes,' David said. 'It's quite different to skiing, but I think I'm getting the hang of it. I quite like it, actually.'

'But it's dark outside,' Lorna reminded him.

'André can find his way through the forest blindfolded.'

'But aren't there bears?' she wanted to know, with a plaintive glance in Roberto's direction, silently begging his support.

He didn't appear to be listening.

André was laughing and shaking his head. 'No problem, Madame Barrett. I take fine care of Monsieur David. We only get lost one time.'

He laughed and slapped David on the shoulder. But David wasn't laughing. When he finally did straighten and turn to face Lorna, his smile was strained. He couldn't seem to look her in the eye, and glanced at his wristwatch, though the clock on the mantelshelf was plain enough to see.

'Not long now,' he announced. 'At midnight the old Basque Christmas tradition takes place. They are out there now, placing torches on the track leading from the forest to the village squares to show Olentzero the way.'

Lorna's head shot up. 'Olentzero?'

How could she have forgotten? According to Basque legend, at midnight, Olentzero comes down through the forest and delivers his presents to the children of all the villages around.

'People are already collecting in the

square around a huge bonfire,' David told her. 'It's all very colourful. The men are decorating a huge fir tree and the women are dishing out mulled wine and those sugary little cakes.'

'The children, too, are there,' André added, his eyes suddenly twinkling with the memory of his own childhood that was not so long ago. 'They are always too excited to sleep on Christmas Eve, eh, Roberto?'

'*Oui, mon ami*,' Roberto said. 'It is the most important time of the year for the children.' He paused, then went on, 'Is my wife out there with the others, André?'

'She is there, Roberto.' André glanced at Lorna and gave an awkward smile. 'And Mixel and Joseba are with Simon.'

'That is good. I am glad,' said Roberto.

★　★　★

Lorna's instinct was to jump up and go in search of her son. She wanted to protect Simon more than anything else. It would be too cruel if he were hurt now, on top of everything else he had suffered lately.

'Lorna, he'll be fine.' David, on detecting her small, involuntary movement, gripped her arms. 'Trust me, sweetheart.'

Lorna drew in a deep breath and forced a smile. How she still adored this man! He was everything she could ask for, and more. And yet, seeing Max again after all these years had put a dull edge around her feelings for David. She looked upon him now more as a much-loved friend or brother than as a potential husband. Perhaps that was how it had always been, and she had fooled herself into thinking it could be something more.

'Oh, David, I'm scared,' she whispered, sinking against his damp chest and breathing in the wet sheep smell rising from his woollen pullover. The wool felt coarse and prickled her cheek, but she felt safe there in his arms.

'There's nothing to be scared about,'

he said into the top of her head. 'Olentzero is a magical being of the forest only to the children. The adults know that he is nothing more than a charcoal maker who makes toys, carrying on the legend of ancient times. In other words, he's just a man doing a job that comes around once a year.'

'But Olentzero is also Max,' Lorna reminded him. 'He's my husband, David, and he doesn't want to acknowledge the fact. Nor does he accept the fact that he has a son. A fine, wonderful son he should be so proud of.'

'Everything is going to be all right, Lorna.'

'I wish I had your confidence,' she said, 'but I can't see a happy ending to this.'

★   ★   ★

David let go of her and began to pace the room. He paced once, twice, three times, and then he spun on his heel and faced her again, his expression firm and determined.

'Sweetheart, I've done all I can to make this work. If it doesn't and everything ends up in pieces — well, I'll still be there to pick up those pieces and hold them together with all the love I can muster.'

'Oh, David! How will you ever forgive me for all this?'

In answer, he planted a kiss on Lorna's forehead. 'There's nothing to forgive,' he told her gently. 'Whatever happens, just remember that I'll always love you.' His smile was bright, but it did not reach his eyes, where a wretchedness had locked itself in.

'Now, I really must go and change into some dry clothes,' he said, leaving the room with meaningful glances at Roberto and André that Lorna could not fathom.

★   ★   ★

At five minutes before midnight, the shout went up. It seemed to Lorna that the whole village erupted. A great wave of raised voices came rushing from the high trail that was hidden by the thick growth of fir trees. It travelled swiftly down between flaming torches and beacons and burst into a deafening chorus in the village square.

'Olentzero! Olentzero! Olentzero!'

The great man of Basque legend was on his way.

'Shall we join them?' David asked, holding out Lorna's coat and scarf.

Lorna nodded. She couldn't trust herself to speak. If she didn't go out there and see her husband play this very important, magical role, she might regret it for evermore. She wanted to be there, not only for her own benefit, but also for Simon's. Heaven only knew what he was feeling right then.

She needn't have worried, for as David helped her on with her coat, the door was flung wide, allowing a soft flurry of snowflakes to enter on an icy blast of wind.

'Mum! Mum, he's here!' Simon's cheeks were burning as he stumbled in his haste to fetch her. 'Olentzero . . . my dad! You've got to come!'

'You too, David,' he said. 'Please?'

'You go on ahead, Simon,' David said. 'I'll follow behind with Roberto.'

'Don't worry about me,' said Roberto, from the depths of his mother's sofa.

'Aren't you coming?' Lorna asked.

'Perhaps it is the accident, but I am feeling very old this evening.'

'Oh, but you've got to come!' It was Simon who rushed over to the Frenchman's side and started pulling on his arm, making Roberto wince. 'Mixel and Joseba are there and all the other children. You can't not be there, Monsieur Lafon. They'll never forgive you.'

Roberto shrugged to sit up, and then he got slowly and painfully to his feet. He leaned on Simon and walked with him out into the crowded village square. David came up behind with a thick quilt, which he draped about the Frenchman's shoulders.

*   *   *

The first sign of movement was a figure that emerged from the darkness of the trees high up on the hillside. It was a young man on skis, making a swift descent, carrying a flaming torch in one hand.

'Olentzero! Olentzero!'

His cries were almost drowned out by the roar of the waiting crowd. Lorna caught Simon's anxious glance and smiled encouragingly at him. She was praying that this night would not end in disaster, but her faith at that moment seemed to be without substance.

Desperate for the physical and moral support of another human body, she leaned against David. His arm went around her in an automatic response, something he had done so many times in the past. Normally, it gave her a warm feeling, but this time it made her feel that she was taking part in some kind of betrayal. In a few short minutes she would again be face to face with

Max, or Olentzero as he was now. Whatever he wanted to call himself, he was still her husband. Nothing could ever change that.

The noise level dropped gradually to a murmur, and then there was an electrified silence as people held their breath and waited for the sound and the sight of Olentzero.

'Listen!' Simon's voice had risen to a squeak in his excitement.

'Hush, *petit*!' Roberto told him. 'Olentzero must arrive in silence.'

Then Lorna heard what Simon had heard. The faint musical sound of a bell jingling in the distance. Its silvery tones got louder and louder. Something moved out of the shadows, a dark, bulky silhouette that gradually took on shape and form as it advanced down the torch-lit slope.

Lorna's chest grew tight and her breathing became difficult as the silhouette broke into recognisable shapes. A donkey, with silver bells hanging from its harness, pulled a sled overflowing with the products of the charcoal maker's labour. But it wasn't coal for the fires that filled the sled. Tonight, the sled was full of toys carved from the pinewood of the forest.

And walking beside the head of Prunelle was the tall, broad-shouldered figure of the famed Olentzero. Although his face was hidden by a large, flat black beret and his body beneath a great cape that reached to his feet, the man walked tall and proud.

He reached the centre of the village and stood, arms raised, beckoning, like some mystical, magical god.

Lorna's heart clenched, then beat uncomfortably fast in her chest. She felt David's hand in the small of her back, pushing her forward, urging her to stay close to Simon, who was forging his way through the throng of people gathered there.

'Keep with him,' he whispered in her ear.

Children of all ages were milling around their hero. One by one, they received a carved toy from Olentzero. He didn't speak a word, but his gestures were kindly as he stroked heads and touched cheeks and shoulders and hands.

Lorna stood behind her son, so close that she could feel the beat of his heart, sense the tension he was under as the children gave thanks for their presents and ran back to their parents to show them what Olentzero had given them.

★   ★   ★

On a nearby hilltop a church bell called everyone to midnight mass. People drifted away. In a very short time, the only people left in the square, apart from Olentzero feeding his donkey, were Roberto and his family with Lorna, David and Simon.

Lorna saw Michel's young wife, Carla, break away from the family group and approach Olentzero. She stopped in her tracks and gazed at the back of the man in the cape who was now turning his donkey-cart in preparation for their return journey to the cottage in the forest.

'He hasn't got anything for me,' Simon said, his face turning up to Lorna's in absolute misery.

Carla heard him and her eyes flashed, but then she was calling out to the departing Basque Santa Claus. The tone of her voice had a touch of sarcasm to it.

'Olentzero! You have forgotten the little English boy!'

Olentzero's footsteps faltered. He turned. As he looked up, the flare from a nearby torch lit up his face. Lorna looked upon it and gasped.

The man who stood there, bathed in torchlight, was not Maxwell Barrett. It was someone Lorna had not seen before. A large Basque, about the same age as Max, but his eyes were like polished jet, his hair long and curled, his beard black and full.

'You're not my father!' Simon yelled. 'Who are you?'

'*Je suis Olentzero!*'

'No, you can't be!' Simon insisted, shaking his head, tears splashing on Lorna's hands as she tried to hold him back. 'Where's my father? What have you done with him?'

The big stranger stared uncomprehendingly at first, then a slow smile spread across his rugged face. One arm came up and he pointed at a light in an upstairs window of the Lafon farmhouse.

'There, *petit*,' he said. 'There is your gift for Noel.'

And as he pointed, the air was filled with the wistful sound of a violin. Lorna heard her son's fractured sobbing as he broke away from her and ran for the house.

'Well, Lorna, what are you waiting for?' David spoke softly behind her.

'I don't understand,' she gasped. 'What's happening?'

'Just a touch of magic.'

'Oh, David!' She stemmed the sob that rose in her throat. 'Oh, I'm so confused. I don't know what to do.'

'You know what to do, Lorna.'

'But . . . but suppose . . . '

David touched a finger to her lips.

'Go to him. Go to him with my blessing.'

Max Remembers

Lorna found Simon standing, statue-like, at the bottom of the stairs of the Lafon house. He had a foot on the first step and one hand gripped the banister so tightly his knuckles were white. He was visibly trembling.

'Oh, Simon . . . ' she murmured. 'Sweetheart, it's all right.'

'I know,' he whispered back to her, but still he did not move.

Above their heads the music carried on, the notes reaching a feverish pitch, and yet there was an uncertainty about them. She did not have to be told that Max had not touched a violin for years. His playing was hesitant, some of the notes not quite reaching the perfection for which he had been famous. During his time here in the Iraty forest he had lived with Nature, made charcoal and carved toys. But he had not, she was sure, practised the music that had been his life until he had been lost to the world.

'Do you think he really likes me?' Simon's voice rasped out hoarsely.

'Oh, Simon, how could he not like you!' Lorna exclaimed, and saw him brush away a stray tear. The sight of him like this, knowing how he must be feeling, was tearing her apart.

'Did you fall out before he went away?'

Lorna was taken aback by his question.

'What makes you think that, sweetheart?'

He shrugged and she saw his bottom lip quiver.

'I thought that maybe you'd had a fight — you know — and that was why he never came back.'

Lorna shook her head. 'No, Simon, it wasn't like that. Your father and I were very much in love.'

As she spoke, she was remembering that last day back in England at the beginning of the war, remembering how frightened she had felt as she said her goodbyes to Max. He had looked so young and handsome and oh, so vulnerable. Deep down inside, she knew he was afraid, yet he was determined to do what was expected of him, like all the other brave servicemen. Like it or not, scared or not, they were ready to serve their King and country, hopeful that their contribution to the war would lead to a better world.

'Stop looking so worried,' he had said, brushing her tears away with his thumbs, kissing the tip of her nose and hugging her so tightly she could hardly breathe. 'I'll come back. I promise. Nothing will ever keep me away from you.'

'How can you be so sure, Max?' she had wanted to know, clinging on to him for dear life even as the guard was calling for the last passengers to board the train. 'I don't want to lose you. I can't lose you.'

He had held her at arms' length,

those mesmeric blue eyes of his holding her gaze, piercing through to her very soul.

'You won't lose me, my darling. No matter what happens, I'll find my way back to you. I couldn't bear not to lay eyes on you ever again.'

Then he had kissed her so tenderly, his lips brushing hers like the soft wings of a butterfly.

Not to lay eyes on her . . . Lorna drew in a breath and placed a hand over her mouth so that her son should not see how deeply moved she was.

Max was now blind. Even if he had come back, he would never have been able to see her again. He was, however, still the same person inside, still the man she had fallen in love with.

And she was the same woman he had married and made promises to. And he had never been a man to break his promises. Better not to make a promise, he would say, unless you knew that you could keep it, no matter what.

'Come on, Simon,' Lorna said now,

taking a grip on her emotions, and an even firmer grip on her son. 'Let's go and see your father, shall we? I think this is something we need to do together. I've got the courage to do it, if you have. Ready?'

'Yes,' Simon whispered, and then they were climbing the stairs together.

Max was in a room at the top of the stairs. The door was open a crack, spilling out yellow light on to the landing and on the two people standing there.

Simon pressed tightly into his mother's side, so tightly that she could feel his body shaking. His small hand gripped hers even tighter as she reached out and gave the door a push with the tips of her fingers. It moved a few inches and they looked in.

* * *

The man the people of Mendibel knew as Olentzero was standing in the centre of the room, his back to the door, playing the violin. As he played, his body swayed slightly to the rhythm of the music. The fingers of his left hand deftly found the positions of the chords on the strings, while the right hand wielded the bow, drawing it down, up, tilting it this way and that.

Lorna hesitated no longer. She gave Simon a push into the room, following him as the door swung open all the way, giving a plaintive creak. The violinist ceased to play and slowly lowered his instrument.

'Who is there?' he demanded, his voice deep and strong, yet tinged with a strange uneasiness.

'Max,' she said. 'It's me . . . Lorna . . . and Simon . . . your son.'

There was a further unbearable silence. Simon hung back nervously. Lorna pushed him further into the room.

'I know you can't see, Max,' she said, her voice catching in her throat, 'but I also know that you do remember me. I don't know why you're pretending you don't, but I beg you . . . please don't reject us. Simon has spent his whole life believing that you were still alive, hoping to find you one day. Max, he wants you to be proud of him. And you would be, if you got to know him. We created something wonderful, you and I. Please . . . don't throw that away.'

Max felt for the table that was in front of him. He put down the violin and turned to face them. His hair had been trimmed, his beard was gone. His clothes were those of a peasant, a country person. It could have been anybody, but it wasn't. It was Maxwell Barrett's eyes that stared directly into Lorna's. Even though he was blind, she knew that he was, in his mind, seeing her.

'Don't be too harsh in your judgement of me,' he said.

'So,' she said. 'You do remember.'

He shook his head. 'Not everything, but . . . the minute I heard your voice, back there in the forest . . . your face flashed through my mind. I couldn't cope with it. It was like a dream I knew I had experienced before, and yet . . . '

The broad shoulders shrugged as he spread his hands, as Gallic a gesture as any Frenchman would make. Lorna wanted to rush to him, take him in her arms, tell him that everything would be all right. But she couldn't. She had to let him speak first.

'Are you really my father?' Simon asked in a whisper.

Max's dark brows lowered, his eyes following the sound of Simon's voice. 'Is that you, boy? The boy who got himself lost in my forest?'

Simon stared at him. Lorna saw his eyes brimming with unshed tears. She looked from one to the other of them, wishing she could embrace them both.

'Max, Simon is your son . . . *our* son,' she said, struggling to keep from disintegrating into little pieces on the floor before him. 'I found out that I was pregnant shortly after you left. I wrote to you, but before I could post the letter I got a telegram saying that your plane was missing and that all on board were believed to be dead.'

Max's fingers searched for a chair, found one, and he sank into it, letting his head fall into his hands.

'And we *were* dead,' he said. 'To all intents and purposes.'

'Didn't you ever want to go back home, Max?' Lorna asked, unable to keep the hurt from her voice.

'What did I have to go back to? I could remember nothing. For months, years, there was just a blank in my mind. I had no identity. Everything I possessed had been lost in the crash. Lost, or . . . ' He fingered his arm and she saw the trace of a scar. 'Burned.'

'You must have wondered, Max,' she said, 'about what you had left behind in England.'

'For a short time, yes, but it nearly drove me mad. I could remember nothing, so I decided it was best not to try. I had to make a new life for myself here in the Pyrenees where I had friends and a family, of a sort.'

'Roberto and . . . Carla?'

'Ah! Of course, you have met the beautiful Carla.'

'How do you know she's beautiful, Max, if you can't see her?'

He gave a smile. 'Because everybody tells me she is beautiful. She herself tells me she is beautiful. However, what I see is a troubled young woman who imagines herself to be in love with Olentzero. A man with mystical powers who might be persuaded to take her away from this place and her memories of the war.'

'And will you?'

'She is the wife of my best friend, the man I owe my life to. What do you think?'

'I think that there are men who wouldn't take that into account.'

'Then you don't know me as well as you imagine . . . Lorna.'

As he said her name for the first time, the bright blue eyes flashed in her direction and she could have sworn that he could see her and was reading everything she had in her mind and her heart.

★　★　★

Lorna felt Simon move restlessly against her and felt angry on behalf of her son. 'Simon thought you might have a present for him, but there was nothing,' she told Max. 'How do you think he feels right now, being forgotten in front of all the French children you favoured?'

Simon sniffed and wiped his sleeve across his eyes. 'It's all right,' he said. 'I don't suppose you had time to make me anything.'

Max was visibly moved. He rose from his chair and held out his arms in Simon's direction. 'Come here, boy,' he commanded, and Simon moved forward to stand close to the man he had never known, yet always loved.

'I don't want presents,' he said. 'I just want you. Mum's going to marry David when they get back to England. I

265

suppose they'll have other children one day . . . '

'Simon!' Lorna called out, wanting him to stop; he was telling Max too much.

Max's hands rested on the boy's shoulders for an instant, and then his fingers fluttered about Simon's face, tracing the fine features that were so like his own. He stroked the boy's head. 'David is a good man, Simon,' he said. 'He will be a good father to you.'

'But I don't want him to be my father. You're my father.'

'I didn't even know that you existed,' Max said gently.

'Max . . . ' Lorna wasn't quite sure what she had been about to say, but Max held up a hand.

'I do have a present for you, Simon,' he said, reaching round to the table behind him and taking up once more the violin and bow. 'This violin. It was once my whole life. One day I would like to hear that your playing on it could charm the angels. Will you promise me that, eh?'

'But what are you going to play?'

Max's face was expressionless, but the blind eyes were dark with emotion. 'You heard me play just now, Simon. I have lost the talent everyone said I had. There is no place in my life now for . . . for music. I am a simple charcoal maker who carves presents for the local children every year at Christmas. I am their Santa Claus.'

'But you're my father . . . ' Simon turned and placed himself squarely before Lorna, crying unashamedly now, but still determined to get through to these two adults who were causing him so much pain. 'Mum! Tell him! He *is* my father.'

Lorna hugged her son tightly. 'Simon, please . . . ' she said, her eyes flashing between her son and the man she loved so deeply it cut into her like a knife. 'I need to talk to Max . . . to your father. Alone. Would you leave us, please, just for a few minutes? There are things your father and I need to say to one another.'

★　★　★

Simon went to stand before Max. He stared up at him and tugged at his jacket. 'Olentzero?' he said.

'Yes, son?'

Simon took a deep breath and held it for a very long time before he felt able to speak. 'Olentzero, you can do magic. All the children in the village have told me how you have performed miracles . . .'

'Ah, Simon, I'm just a man. A man with eyes that do not see. In fact, what a poor specimen I am. You are much better off without me, you and your mother.'

'No! That's not true! If you could see Mum, you would know . . .'

'Know what, Simon?'

'She's ever so pretty, just like she was on your wedding photographs. And . . . and . . .'

'Yes . . . ?'

'And she still loves you. If she didn't love you she would have married David a long time ago.'

'Is that so?'

'Yes, and if you don't come back home with us right now, she really will marry him and she won't be happy.'

'Don't you like David, then?'

'Yes, but he's not my father! He's not you!'

Lorna heard Max's sigh. 'You should leave us now, Simon. There are things that cannot be discussed in front of a child.'

'All right,' Simon said, 'I'll go, but you can't not come back home with us, you really can't!'

Simon glanced in Lorna's direction as he walked slowly out of the room. She gave him an uncertain smile as he passed by her and closed the door behind him.

★   ★   ★

'Has he gone?' Max said.

'Yes,' Lorna said, in a voice so faint that she thought he wouldn't hear, but he had.

'Good.' Max nodded. 'He's a good boy, this son of ours.'

'So you do accept that he is your son?'

'How could I do otherwise, Lorna? If you say it's so, then it's so.'

'Max . . . ' She held her breath for a moment. 'I would have liked to tell you that there has never been another man in my life — and there wasn't. Not for a very long time, long after I believed you to be dead. Then I met David and . . . '

'And you fell in love.' Max bowed his head. 'I can't blame you for that. I like the fellow. And he loves you very much.'

'Did he tell you that?'

'He didn't have to, Lorna. I can read it in his voice, feel it in the air he breathes. And he loves you so much he's willing to give you up if it will make you happy.'

Lorna stared at Max, not knowing where this conversation was going, not knowing which direction her heart would take.

She let out a long sigh and sat down,

staring at her clasped hands on the table before her.

'I'm not going to ask you to decide between us,' Max said, moving away from her as if he could not bear to be so close. 'That would be unfair. Besides, I think I know what you would do, and all for the wrong reasons.'

'Max, I . . . '

'No, Lorna, please listen to me.' He had to wait a few long seconds before he could trust himself to continue. 'You have made a good life for yourself and the boy. I have played no part in it, but David has. For years you thought I was dead, and, in a way, the Maxwell Barrett that you knew *is* dead. I will not impose myself on you, Lorna. You deserve better than a blind, ex-musician for a husband.'

Lorna jumped to her feet. 'No, Max . . . please don't send me away . . . please.'

He gave a shake of his head. 'I couldn't stand your pity, my darling. And that's why I must ask you to divorce me.'

'No! No, I can't! Max, don't do this to me!' Lorna was trying to hold on to a heart that threatened to disintegrate into a million pieces. 'I realise that it won't be easy for you, not after all this time, but we had something special once. Has your life changed so much that you can't remember what we meant to each other?'

'Oh, I do know now, believe me,' Max said, his voice frighteningly firm. 'But Lorna, my darling, I am not the man you married. I can never again be that man.'

'We could try, Max . . . work something out . . . ' Lorna stopped. Why was she pleading like this when he plainly didn't want her? And yet . . . wasn't he the one man in the world who was worth pleading for?

She rounded the table and stood close to him. She took his hands and guided them up to her face. The hands that she had once adored were no longer smooth. They were the hands of a charcoal maker, a carpenter. But they were still good, strong hands. Max's hands.

'Lorna, don't . . . don't do this to me.'

He was trying to draw away, but she held on fast.

'You don't need eyes to see me, Max. Feel my face. See it through your fingertips, the way you see your pieces of wood.'

'How could I ever have forgotten you,' he murmured brokenly, pulling his hands away. 'You were the first thing I remembered when I got my memory back — and even when I had no memory, your face haunted my dreams. I didn't know who you were — not until I heard your voice that day in the forest and so many pieces fell into place.'

'It was the most scary, most wonderful, thing I have ever experienced. As soon as I heard you speak I knew that somehow my heart had always belonged to you. And always would.'

Oh, what she would not give just to

feel his arms around her the way she used to. The love was still there. It had never left.

'Come back to England with me, Max. Get to know your son. You'll be so proud to be his father.'

Max gave a short, dry laugh. 'The problem is, I can't make him proud of me. What use would I be to either of you, without my sight? The world has gone on without me. No-one will remember the great violinist, Maxwell Barett. No, Lorna, you must take Simon back to England. Go back and marry David. And forget me.'

'You always did have a stubborn streak, Max!' she shouted at him through sobs of despair. 'Do you really think the world has forgotten you? Well, you're wrong. And you can still make beautiful music. You've just proved that.'

'Lorna . . . please, my dear, sweet love . . . ' His voice broke and he turned his head, but not before she saw his eyes brimming with tears.

'Oh, Max!'
'Go! For God's sake, go, Lorna!'

★ ★ ★

She stood for a long time, watching him, helpless, her shoulders sagging, her heart breaking. Then she became aware of David standing behind her, David's hands on her shoulders, and David's warm breath on her neck.

And the man she had known and loved as her husband for so long, now seemed suddenly smaller and vulnerable, as he sat slumped at the table, his shoulders shaking with emotion.

She wanted to tell him, over and over again, that she still loved him, still wanted him, but she couldn't. He wouldn't listen. All she could do was leave him there, as he had asked her to do.

Leave him in the dark, loveless world he had chosen.

A Touch Of Magic

'Will somebody please pinch me!' Lorna said, as she bustled about, wondering where the taxi was. 'I still can't believe that this is happening.'

'What can't you believe?'

Lorna's sister, Rachel, was touching up her makeup in the mirror. They had been conducting this two-way conversation for over an hour now, while getting ready for the big event of the evening.

'Well, you know ... this evening.' Lorna thought that if the taxi didn't arrive soon she was going to have a panic attack.

'Yes, I know,' Rachel grinned at Lorna and gave her a hug. 'We're all so happy, Lorna. And proud. You must be too.'

Lorna gave a nervous laugh. Oh, yes, she was certainly that. Yet there was still a tiny corner of disbelief niggling away

276

at her, telling her that none of this could possibly be true. It was a dream and she would wake up and be back in France with David and Simon. And Olentzero would come and give them all gifts he had carved with his own hands.

But that had been four years ago.

How must Simon be feeling, she wondered? What if he got his fingers all in a knot and made a mess of things? What if he was so nervous he couldn't bring himself to perform?

He was such a sensitive boy. However, she had to admit that in the last two years he had grown and matured. At fifteen, he was surprisingly manly in many ways. And in other ways, he was still her little boy, her baby, though she went to great pains not to treat him as such. It was so hard at times to stand back and give him the space to breathe and find his independence.

'What's going through your head to give you that dreamy expression?' Rachel asked.

'I was just thinking that I have David to thank for pretty much everything.'

'Don't you just! Lovely man that he is.' Rachel looked fondly across to where David was struggling with his bow tie.

'Shouldn't the taxi be here by now?' Lorna looked at her watch as if she hadn't checked the time only minutes before.

Her sister gave her a pained look. 'How many more times are you going to ask about that blasted taxi?' she said. 'It'll be on time.'

'Are you sure?' Lorna was rushing about barefoot looking for the shoes she had just decided against, but that now seemed to be the best choice after all.

'For goodness' sake, calm down, Lorna!' David walked across the hotel room and replaced Rachel in front of the mirror. 'Blast these bow tie jobs. I can never get the things straight. Can one of you girls help me out here?'

'Don't look at me,' Lorna said. 'My fingers are shaking so much, your tie would end up looking like a piece of tangled string.'

'Here, let me have a go,' Rachel said.

'I think my watch must have stopped,' Lorna said, frowning down at the slim gold-framed face of her wristwatch. She tapped at it anxiously.

'No, it hasn't,' Rachel said. 'The hands haven't had enough time to move on from the last time you looked.'

'I hope Mum and Dad won't be late,' Lorna said, gazing out of the window into the darkness of the December night.

'Of course they won't,' David said. 'Everything's going to be just fine,' and he gave her one of those brotherly hugs that always made her feel better.

'Look, Lorna, the taxi will be here at any minute, you'll see. Parents and grandparents will not let Simon down, any more than Simon will let them down, or us.'

'Have a small gin and tonic or something to settle your nerves,' Rachel suggested, investigating the courtesy bar with interest.

'I don't think that's a good idea!' said

Lorna, at the same time that David exclaimed, 'She really shouldn't!'

'Oh, yes, I forgot.' Rachel looked apologetically at Lorna's swollen stomach. 'But maybe just a teaspoonful of brandy wouldn't hurt.'

'No thanks, Rachel,' Lorna said. 'I'm not going to take any risks with this baby. Besides, it would go straight to my head and then I'd make a fool of myself.'

'Oh, all right,' Rachel said. 'I suppose I shouldn't, either, but my friend Mavis was tipsy right through all of her pregnancies. Mind you, she has four children who are not the brightest stars in the firmament.'

The two women laughed. Being twins, they had always been close, always done things together. So it wasn't surprising that they had both fallen pregnant at the same time.

'I think,' David said, peering out of the window and letting in a blast of ice-laden air, 'that our taxi has finally arrived. Shall we go?'

★ ★ ★

'Dear David,' Rachel whispered to Lorna as they walked to the lift behind him. 'He hates it when we talk about girlie things, doesn't he?'

'Oh, he'll be all right,' Lorna replied. What else could she have said? All the same, she hoped that David *was* all right.

'What's wrong?' Rachel said. 'You've gone all serious.'

'Nothing's wrong,' Lorna said, taking her sister's arm and squeezing it. 'In fact, everything's so right. I'm just a little afraid that I might be too happy, that's all.'

'Nobody can be too happy. Look at me! Happy as a skylark and I could stand more of the stuff without any problem at all.'

'I'm so glad, Rachel.'

★ ★ ★

The Royal Albert Hall was a sight to behold, festively lit and decorated for that evening's special charity concert. It glowed and sparkled like a fairy grotto. The vast auditorium was overflowing with holly, scarlet poinsettia and creamy pale Christmas roses.

'It's breathtaking!' Lorna said, as David, with her on one side and Rachel on the other, walked them to their reserved places.

They were recognised, of course. First by friends and family, then by other members of the assembling audience, who gave a short burst of applause. Those closest to them called out greetings, congratulations and good wishes.

Lorna was getting used to all the attention by now, but poor Rachel grew crimson with embarrassment. She sat down quickly in her seat and buried her head in her programme. 'I didn't expect that,' she whispered to Lorna.

Lorna laughed and squeezed her sister's hand, but she, too, was feeling just a little overcome by the exuberance of their reception.

'It used to be like this all the time,' she said. 'I hated it at first, but then I realised it was something I had to live with. It wasn't until it stopped . . . you know, with the war and everything . . . that I really appreciated it. Only then, it was too late. I'd almost forgotten how exciting my life had been.'

'There's a limit to how much excitement I can take,' Rachel said, 'but I expect I could get used to it.'

★   ★   ★

The concert was being held in aid of blind war veterans. It had been young Simon's idea and he had taken it upon himself to write to the Royal London Philharmonic orchestra seeking their help and support. The response had been so generous it had knocked everyone, Simon included, sideways.

Well-known show-business personalities, too, had agreed to perform, and they had ended up with an impressive list of artistes willing to give freely of their time in order to raise the funds which would go towards refurbishing a hospital in Kent and turning it into a School for the Blind.

Lorna scanned the crowds. People were taking their seats. They looked as eager and as excited as she felt. The orchestra was tuning up. Trombones and tubas, saxophones and violins, were competing against one another in a cacophony of sound.

Simon was somewhere backstage, she knew. A sudden flurry of butterflies invaded her stomach. They had managed to see him briefly, but there wasn't time to spend more than a minute hugging him and wishing him luck. He had looked flushed with excitement, but not nearly as nervous as Lorna had expected.

'I can't see my parents,' Lorna said, swivelling round in her seat.

'There they are,' David told her, patting her arm and indicating a row on the other side of the aisle. 'My mother

284

and my aunt are there, too. It's hard to tell which of the women is wearing the silliest hat.'

'What's my father doing?' Lorna asked, straining her neck, but not quite seeing her family.

'Smoking like a chimney and trying to look as if he wished he were somewhere else.'

'Typical! He hates this kind of thing, but if he missed tonight he would never forgive himself.'

'He's studying the programme as if it's a menu and the prices are too high.'

'What on earth makes you say that?' Lorna laughed.

'The back of his neck is red.'

'Poor Dad.' Lorna exchanged amused glances with her sister. 'He always turns the colour of a turkey when he's anxious or angry.'

'Well,' Rachel said, 'I can assure you that he's anything but angry tonight.'

'You're right there,' David said. 'This must be the happiest gathering since the Armistice celebrations.'

'Isn't it time they got started?' Rachel sounded as anxious as Lorna, but then, her favourite nephew was about to make his debut on the stage tonight. And it wasn't just any stage. Nor was it just any audience. There were plenty of influential people here tonight. There was every chance of Simon's great talent being heard and picked up by an impresario.

'Won't it be wonderful if Simon makes it as a professional violinist?' Lorna said. 'You know, follow in his father's footsteps?'

'Yes, wonderful,' David said. 'And I'm sure he will, if that's what he really wants.'

'Oh, he wants to all right,' Lorna said with infinite pride, as the first strains of the introductory overture started up and a hush fell over the great hall.

The first half of the concert, although enjoyable enough, seemed very long. Possibly, Lorna thought, because she was so impatient for the much-awaited finale that meant so much to her, so much to all of them.

★ ★ ★

During the interval, Rachel excused herself to go in search of the cloak-rooms.

'Would you like me to come with you?' David was already on his feet.

Rachel shook her head. 'No. You stay here and keep Lorna company or she'll explode with anxiety.'

They all laughed at that and she waddled off happily.

'My sister!' Lorna smiled after her. 'I never thought she'd take to mother-hood, but she seems to be loving it.'

'Yes, she does, doesn't she?'

'David,' Lorna said, 'I don't think I shall ever be able to thank you enough for what you've done for Simon . . . and for me.'

'Nonsense! It's all been worth it to see you both so happy.'

'Oh, David, you're such a good person.'

Rachel returned to them, chattering joyfully about the celebrities she had bumped into. 'Isn't it wonderful, all this fame?' she said. 'It was all I could do not to ask for autographs, and then I reminded myself that I was related to the most famous person here tonight!'

'Oh, Rachel, you are an idiot!' Lorna said affectionately. 'But a very nice one, isn't she, David?'

'The best in her class.'

'He's just saying that because . . . ' Rachel suddenly lowered her voice to an excited whisper. 'The lights are going down. This is it, Lorna!'

David reached out and gripped Lorna's left hand and Rachel's right. The moment they had all been waiting for was upon them and the tension they felt was almost palpable.

There was a roll of drums. The master of ceremonies walked out on to the stage. Lorna held her breath and her heart did a somersault as the man made his very special announcement.

'Ladies and gentlemen. This is what we have all been waiting for . . . Not just this evening, but for too many years.

And I won't keep you in suspense any longer. The star of our show needs no introduction. All of us here know him and love him for the brave and talented person he is. I give you, ladies and gentlemen, Mr Maxwell Barrett.'

The hall erupted, but all Lorna was aware of was the tall, broad-shouldered figure of her husband being led out on to the stage by Simon. Each of them were holding a violin.

Clean-shaven and handsome once more, Max was smiling the biggest, proudest smile Lorna had ever seen. Simon looked understandably nervous and self-conscious, but that, she knew, would disappear. He was only fifteen, but he was every inch his father's son.

Max acknowledged the uproarious welcome of his audience, his hand staying firmly on Simon's shoulder, which was almost as high as his own now. The boy had grown tall and sturdy in the last two years.

'Thank you, my friends!' Max had to wait a long time before he could speak, and there was a noticeable quiver in his voice.

There was further uproar as members of the audience cried out to Max, urging him to play the much-loved piece that had made him so popular.

'Play the Bruch, Mr Barrett! Play the Bruch!'

Max's smile grew even wider as he held up his hands to silence them. 'I won't disappoint you,' he said. 'I'll play the Bruch Violin Concerto . . . ' There was a short burst of applause and some hearty cheers, then he continued: 'But I am going to dedicate it to some very special people. People without whom I would not be here tonight. And most important of all, my son is going to accompany me.'

'I want you to welcome Simon Barrett. This is his first appearance in public as a violinist, so be gentle with him . . . and with me.'

Another deafening roar from the audience drowned his last words. Max waited for the noise to die down, and then he turned, as if instinct directed him, and seemed to look directly at Lorna. His smile was soft and full of love.

'This is for you, my love,' he said, and both he and Simon bowed to her.

Then the orchestra started to play Bruch's First Violin Concerto and everyone was immersed in the exquisite sound of two violins playing in tandem. Father and son, matching note for note.

The duo played as none before them had played, every note laden with emotion. The music reached its height in a magnificent crescendo, then calmed, and gave way to a wistful passage.

Simon, almost as tall as his father, lowered his instrument and took a step back. His eyes were brimming with pride as he allowed Max to continue playing alone. The Bruch had never sounded so beautiful. Lorna felt her heart swell with love for this man and the son he had given her.

On the last note the hall erupted. The audience were up on their feet, frantically clapping, everyone calling out for more.

Lorna's heart was bursting. Tears of happiness welled in her eyes and rolled unchecked down her cheeks. Women in the audience wept openly, while men surreptitiously wiped away a tear. The Maestro was back. Maestro, husband and father, beloved in all his roles.

It seemed like the audience would never stop applauding. They wouldn't be satisfied until Max and Simon had played the Finale again as an encore.

As they finished a second time, this time together, Lorna saw the immense pride in her husband's face. Pride and the trace of a tear on his black lashes, as he put an affectionate arm about his son's shoulders.

She glanced across at David, also on his feet and applauding with the rest of them. David, who had loved her so much that he had given her up in favour of the man she had thought was dead, but was now more alive than he had ever been. David, who had selflessly put that love aside in order to persuade Max to come back home and be the husband and father she had always known he could be.

'Thank you,' she mouthed to him and was met by a small nod and a genuine smile.

★ ★ ★

David and Rachel had married a year ago. They were happy. Anybody could see that. Lorna was sure that their marriage would work, just as she was sure that her future with Max was secure.

She looked at Max now, seeing him acknowledge the appreciation, the adulation, of the audience and her whole being filled to overflowing. The man she loved, had always loved, had been given back to her.

As if he could read her thoughts reaching out to him across the auditorium, Max blew her a kiss and said, 'Merry Christmas, sweetheart!'

Lorna ignored her tears, just as she

ignored the hundreds of people gazing at her. She had eyes only for Max and their wonderful son.

She gave a trembling smile and whispered, 'Merry Christmas, Olentzero.'

THE END

We do hope that you have enjoyed reading this large print book.

Did you know that all of our titles are available for purchase?

We publish a wide range of high quality large print books including:
Romances, Mysteries, Classics
General Fiction
Non Fiction and Westerns

Special interest titles available in large print are:
The Little Oxford Dictionary
Music Book, Song Book
Hymn Book, Service Book

Also available from us courtesy of Oxford University Press:
Young Readers' Dictionary
(large print edition)
Young Readers' Thesaurus
(large print edition)

For further information or a free brochure, please contact us at:
Ulverscroft Large Print Books Ltd.,
The Green, Bradgate Road, Anstey,
Leicester, LE7 7FU, England.
Tel: (00 44) **0116 236 4325**
Fax: (00 44) **0116 234 0205**

DANGEROUS FLIRTATION

Liz Fielding

Rosalind thought she had her life all mapped out — a job she loved, a thoughtful, reliable fiancé . . . what more could she want? How was she to know that a handsome stranger with laughing blue eyes and a roguish grin would burst into her life, kiss her to distraction and turn her world upside down? But there was more to Jack Drayton than met the eye. He offered romance, excitement, and passion — and challenged Rosalind to accept. Dared she?

ROMANTIC LEGACY

Joyce Johnson

Wedding plans in ruins, Briony Gordon immerses herself in her job as senior wine buyer at Lapwings Wine Merchants until a dramatic turn of events forces her to reconsider her future. A substantial legacy from her beloved Grandfather gives her the incentive to explore new possibilities. At Moonwarra winery in Western Australia, Briony finds feuding brothers quarrelling over the Winery's future — a future which gives her a wonderful business opportunity and where she finds true love . . .

CONFLICT OF THE HEART

Dorothy Taylor

A summer job, as live-in nanny, caring for seven-year-old Ellie seems like a dream for Karen Carmichael. But while Ellie proves a delight, her father, archaeologist Neil Oldson is hard to get to know. Karen puts his reserve down to pressure from the looming deadline on the nearby Roman site he is managing. But when valuable finds from the site are stolen, her growing feelings for him are thrown into doubt. Then Karen's life is put in danger.